Syrus Ephraem, James Rendel Harris

Fragments of the Commentary of Ephrem Syrus

upon the Diatessaron

Syrus Ephraem, James Rendel Harris

Fragments of the Commentary of Ephrem Syrus
upon the Diatessaron

ISBN/EAN: 9783337286224

Printed in Europe, USA, Canada, Australia, Japan

Cover: Foto ©Andreas Hilbeck / pixelio.de

More available books at **www.hansebooks.com**

FRAGMENTS OF THE COMMENTARY

OF

EPHREM SYRUS

UPON THE

DIATESSARON.

London: C. J. CLAY AND SONS,

CAMBRIDGE UNIVERSITY PRESS WAREHOUSE,

AVE MARIA LANE.

Glasgow: 263, ARGYLE STREET.

Leipzig: F. A. BROCKHAUS.

New York: MACMILLAN AND CO.

FRAGMENTS OF THE COMMENTARY

OF

EPHREM SYRUS

UPON THE

DIATESSARON

BY

J. RENDEL HARRIS, M.A., D. Litt. (Dubl.)

FELLOW OF CLARE COLLEGE, CAMBRIDGE.

LONDON:

C. J. CLAY AND SONS,

CAMBRIDGE UNIVERSITY PRESS WAREHOUSE,

AVE MARIA LANE.

1895

Cambridge:

PRINTED BY J. AND C. F. CLAY,

AT THE UNIVERSITY PRESS.

PRINTED IN GREAT BRITAIN

PREFACE.

In a recent article in the *Contemporary Review* (August, 1895) I have shown that there is a close and constant dependence of the later Syriac commentators upon the Commentary which Ephrem Syrus made upon Tatian's Diatessaron; and I have found upon a further examination of these writers that it is possible to restore, sometimes exactly and sometimes approximately, large portions of the lost Syriac text of Ephrem, of which, up to the present, no fragment has been produced, and of which no representative is extant except the Armenian translation published by the Venetian fathers. As the recovery of these portions of the lost text not only elucidates the often doubtful meaning of the Armenian version, but also throws much light upon the history and fortunes of the composition, I have thought it worth while to commit the matter to the press in the hope that it will not be valueless to the critic even if a complete copy of the lost Syriac work should ultimately be recovered.

CONTENTS.

CORRIGENDUM.

P. 18, l. 29, for ⟨script⟩ read ⟨script⟩

INTRODUCTION.

THE Commentary of Ephrem Syrus has, for various reasons, hardly met with the welcome and the elucidation which so famous a work deserves. Probably this is due, on the one side, to the fact that it was, until the present pages were written, extant only in Armenian, and the paucity of scholars who are acquainted with that language has reacted upon the subject, and caused a somewhat cold treatment of the book itself; but it is also due, in part, to the odium anti-theologicum which was provoked by the appearance of a work which was supposed, rightly or wrongly, to have an important bearing upon the history of the Canon; so that in some quarters there have been muttered rumours that the work was not rightly ascribed to the great Syrian father whose name it bears, while in other quarters of the critical world, especially those which lie most nearly adjacent to the city of Tübingen, it has been treated with a silence that must be, to the looker-on, who proverbially has the best view of the game, very significant.

Now it is unfortunate that this should be the case; unfortunate, I mean, that so many persons (myself amongst the number) are ignorant of Armenian, and that some persons (amongst whom I sincerely hope not to be included) limit their interest in a great work by the boundary of their theological or anti-theological predilections; and it is the more to be regretted, because the interest of the work does not lie primarily either in the fact that it is in Armenian, or in its possible bearing upon the evolution of the second century Gospels. Ephrem, himself, is a theological star of the first magnitude, and even if he should happen to be one of the worthiest representatives of Catholic orthodoxy, his windows always overlook the fields of the early unorthodox teachers, whom the Church has successively banned, but without the knowledge of whom the Church Historian cannot construct the map of the

Ecclesiastical Empire or interpret the riddles which occur so
constantly in the History of Dogma.

Not only so, but the stones which he throws at the Docetists,
at Marcion, at Bardesanes and others are usually of the nature of
replies; and the stones which had originally been thrown at his
own party can often be found lying under his windows. He loves
repartee, but as repartee requires, to make it intelligible, the
preliminary remarks of the objector, it will be found that often,
in Ephrem's pages, there can be recognized statements which were
taken *ex ore dubitantium*, or have been extracted directly from
heretical works. Marcion has, indeed, perished, but some Marcionite flies (often large ones) are in Ephrem's amber. A careful
critic can often separate the two.

For example, in Ephrem's comment on Luke xi. 27 (ed.
Mösinger, p. 122), the writer expressly tells us that he is quoting
Marcion, and the margin of the MS. tells us that 'all this was
said by Marcion.' The only question then is, how much is rightly
to be included under the marks of quotation. Apparently we
may isolate the following words:

'Blessed shall be the womb that bare thee.' Marcion says "By
these words they only tempted him to see whether he was born
in reality. And where it is said, 'Lo! thy mother and thy
brethren seek thee' the same thing is signified. And further he
gave them his body to eat."

The argument is that the body is a phantasm and the birth
not real. For our Lord did not acknowledge the suggested rela-
tionships to mother and brethren. And Ephrem's reply is that if
our Lord had wished to deny his nativity and human nature, he
would not afterwards have claimed fraternity with disciples who
were but men. And by a happy retort he compares the verse in
which our Lord might be supposed to say 'Why callest thou me
conceived and born' with that other much disputed text 'Why
callest thou me good,' from which the Marcionites were in the
habit of arguing and where Ephrem and others shew great skill
in refuting them.

In another passage he is arguing with those who held with
Marcion that Christ appeared suddenly in the synagogue at
Nazareth, or as Tertullian puts it, that he came *de caelo in
synagogam*. The dispute in such cases did not turn on the
question of the genuineness of the portions of the Gospel which

deal with the Nativity, for the Marcionite had no such account in his gospel; but it turned upon the words 'he went, as his custom was, into the synagogue.' And it was argued, not improperly, by the opponents of Marcion that these words were inconsistent with the theory of a sudden lapse from heaven. Accordingly, as I have elsewhere suggested[1], the text of the Gospel at this point shews signs of having been tampered with in certain copies with a view to meeting the difficulty, either by getting rid of the 'custom' or by proving it to refer to other people or by erasing the words 'where he had been brought up.' Now it is interesting to find that the very words of Marcion on this point are preserved to us by Ephrem. And it appears that Marcion objects to this disputed word 'consuetudo.' The passage is as follows (Mösinger, p. 128):

Matt. xiii. 54. *He came into his own city and taught them in their synagogues....*This was written to confound the Marcionites: [because, that is, by teaching in his *native place* and by teaching *in their synagogues* the scripture implies previous residence and habitual teaching.]...Luke iv. 16. *After these things he entered into their synagogue, as his custom was, on the Sabbath-day.* [Here Marcion is supposed to intervene;] whence arises the custom to him who had only just arrived? He had but just come into Galilee: nor had he [even on the orthodox shewing] begun to preach outside the synagogue, [in which case the custom of preaching would have been established] but he began in the synagogue, (and we must either admit) as their worship requires, that he preached to them concerning their God, [the creator of the world] or else he would have had to preach outside the synagogues. [But if he preached about their God to them then this must have been what provoked their anger; nothing had passed between them before], and his visit to Bethsaida [so, according to Marcion, and *not* Nazareth] was only marked on their side by the suggestion that the physician should heal himself. This is not sufficient to explain their anger and their desire to throw him from the rock. [We must, therefore, allow that he had said things to them about their God, which provoked them, and this must have been the first occasion upon which such things were said.]

To which Ephrem replies (i) that if Christ had been in the habit of preaching against the God of the Old Testament, traces of it would be found elsewhere in the Gospel; (ii) that the very

---

[1] *A Study of Codex Bezae*, p. 232.

words which he used about a prophet being without honour in his own country imply his previous residence among them.

In this way we get glimpses of the character of the disputes between the Marcionite and the Catholic; we can reconstruct something of the argument, and we can collect the leading passages around which the discussion raged. Indeed it will often be found that the texts which Ephrem treats with the greatest fulness and variety are those which relate to the burning questions of the generation or century preceding his own; and the only difficulty lies in determining when he is speaking in his own person, and not quoting or personating a heretic.

Another case which he discusses is that in which the physical body of Christ was denied, for it appears that he enters into an argument with those who held that Christ's body was not natural, but had descended from heaven, perhaps by passing through the Virgin, as water through a tube, according to some Valentinian Gnostics. It is evident from Ephrem that such persons had made use of the expression in the Gospel of John, 'no man hath ascended into heaven except him that descended from heaven'; from which they concluded that Christ descended σωματικῶς from above. And they seem to have confirmed this belief, in Syria, by the use of the primitive translation of the Gospel of John into Syriac, in which we are told (John i. 14) that 'the Word became (or was) *a body* and dwelt among us.' To these Ephrem replies[1]

'You are not to say that the body of Christ descended from heaven...but it was Gabriel who descended from heaven...and therefore it says 'He that descended from heaven.''

And I think we can see the difficulty which arose in the interpretation of the first chapter of John by the naïve admission of another Syriac commentator[2], to whom we shall presently refer, and who is perhaps retailing an actual remark of Ephrem, that the original reading was 'body' but it was changed to 'flesh' in order that people might not suppose that the body descended from heaven[3].

One other instance shall be given of the importance of the Ephrem Commentary for a knowledge of the early heresies. I

---

[1] Mösinger, p. 187.

[2] Isho'dad of Merv.

[3] How characteristic was this translation of σάρξ by 'body' may be seen by studying the text of the Old Syriac Version of the Gospels.

have pointed out elsewhere[1] the meaning of the curious passage[2] in which Ephrem says that the words in Daniel where 'a stone is cut out without hands,' are not the same in meaning as the passage 'Look to the mountain and the valley,' in which case he intimates the male and the female. But here he says 'without hands.'

The explanation of our Lord's birth from a virgin by means of Daniel's stone without hands is, of course, well known, but Ephrem reveals to us the counter text of the Adoptionist who objects to the stone without hands a stone hewn out of a mountain and a valley; he is quoting Isaiah li. 1 as a reference to the Syriac text with Ephrem's comment on it will shew, and hence concludes for a natural birth by the male and the female[3].

It is in this way that we are able to restore the watchwords of early battlefields, and no book will help us to so many of these as Ephrem's Commentary on the Diatessaron. For the study of Marcionism, Gnosticism or Adoptionism, it is of very great value; and deserves, therefore, an edited text and a scientific commentary.

Not less important is the volume for the light that it throws upon the Old Syriac text both of the distinct Gospels and of the Diatessaron. The textual critic will read his Ephrem side by side with the oldest copies of the Syriac text. For if the Ephrem Commentary often throws light upon the early condition of the Syriac text, conversely the early Syriac texts (notably the Lewis text) often throw light upon Ephrem. The recurrence, for example, of some curious word or expression will often shew what was the reading most familiar to Ephrem, even where the verse itself may not be actually quoted, or where, when it was actually quoted, the influence of the later Vulgate text has caused a superficial correction.

For example, in Matt. i. 25, Ephrem's copy of the Diatessaron read 'Sancte habitabat cum ea' as in the Curetonian. Six times Ephrem quotes it directly; but the diffusion of the reading is such that not only does it influence his comments in other places such

---

[1] *Contemp. Rev.* Nov. 1894, p. 669.

[2] Mösinger, p. 22.

[3] Another Adoptionist error is corrected on p. 27, where we are told that the Scripture does not say 'a Saviour who is to become the Lord's Christ, but a Saviour who already is the Lord's Christ.'

as (p. 21) the passage where he says that Joseph was so gentle as not to expel her from the house, *sed cum ea habitaret;* but it even turns up in the objection made by an ideal Adoptionist interlocutor who says (p. 26)

> Nonne ergo conjugium sanctum est, testante
> Apostolo, Thorus eorum sanctum est[1]?

This instance is the more curious, since the Cureton reading was probably intended as an Anti-Adoptionist correction. But the fact is that the reading must have acquired great prevalence, for we find traces of it in later Syriac commentators also.

Or take the passage to which we draw attention on p. 34 (Luke ii. 34), in which from the repeated word *dubitare* we are able to restore the text of Tatian in a place where a later reviser of Ephrem has substituted a reading more in accordance with the Greek.

A very interesting case will be found in the account of our Lord's healing of the leper[2], where Ephrem comments as follows:

Dominus duo pro his duobus ei ostendit, reprehensionem, *cum ei irasceretur,* et misericordiam, cum sanaret. Quia dixit, Si vis, *iratus est*.........Propterea Dominus *per indignationem* monstravit se non ex personarum acceptione sanare...........................
Quare Dominus propter has cogitationes ei *iratus est* et deinceps ei praecepit.........Sed et animadverte non ei, sed leprae Christum *iratum esse.*

The continual play upon the words *iratum esse* shews that the text used by Ephrem had this expression. This is the more important because, as far as I know, up to the present time, the only evidence for such a reading was the Western text (with D, d, a ff[2]) in Mark i. 41, where Codex Bezae has ὀργισθείς. The diffusion of this reading in Syriac as well as in Greco-Latin texts is therefore demonstrated.

Or turn to the passage (Luke i. 6) where Zachary and Elisabeth are said[3] to be 'Immaculati in omni regione sua.' A reference to the foot-note of Mösinger shews that the text should have been printed 'Immaculati in omni habitatione sua'; and a few pages further on the same reading is betrayed where Ephrem says

---

[1] From the fact that Ephrem does not directly reply to this ingenious objection, one is almost tempted to suspect that it is the gloss of an Adoptionist reader.

[2] Mösinger, p. 144.   [3] Mösinger, p. 7.

that it is not proper to criticise persons like Zachary and Elisabeth who are said to have been immaculate 'in omni vitae conditione,' for here again the editor notes that one of his copies reads 'in omni habitatione.' There can be little doubt as to the correct reading; but here the Sinai text comes to our aid, and solves the problem as to what had been puzzling the Armenian scribes, by telling us that Zachary and Elisabeth were 'without blame in all their conversation'; the word which we render 'conversation,' ܟܘܡܪܐ, has been referred to its root which means to 'dwell' or 'inhabit.' We have thus an agreement between the Old Syriac text and that of Tatian in a very free and forcible translation.

But we need not say more on this point, except to add that what is true of Ephrem is also true of later Syriac commentators, especially of those who derive from him. Their comments as well as their texts are to be used in the determination of Old Syriac readings, and a trained ear will often catch the refrain of such readings and be able to separate them from the rest of the passage in which they may be imbedded.

It will, therefore, be admitted that the Ephrem commentary deserves critical editing, with a view to determine something more than the pre-existence, early diffusion and harmonisation of the four Gospels. And this is rendered the more necessary because the Editor of the Latin translation has not given us a scientific text; of the two copies, A and B, which he uses, one is an editorial recension made by a certain Nerses, in which difficulties have been conjecturally got rid of, and texts speculatively improved in such a way that we can only describe the work as in certain passages de-Ephremized. It would have been better to have printed the text merely from the copy A, without any reference to the other copy, than to combine the two, often so as to produce a text of which we can only say that, whatever it is, it is not the text of Ephrem. The first step then in studying the work is to purify it of some of the editorial B-readings and of all the composite A + B readings. I am sorry that my ignorance of Armenian does not permit me to undertake this correction[1]. But, if I cannot do this, I am glad

[1] It will also be necessary to correct a great many of the editor's references to the Old Testament which are demonstrated to be incorrect, as soon as we refer to the Syriac Bible, as well as to correct such lacunae of reference as in the passage

to say that my researches in another direction have been very fruitful. I have set to work to see how much of the original Syriac text may be extant in the shape of Catenae or Commentaries on the Gospel in the Syriac tongue : and the present volume will shew that a great deal is to be gathered from the Syriac commentators both for the knowledge of the Diatessaron and of Ephrem's comment upon it.

Of the writers upon whom I depend those to whom I chiefly refer are Isho'dad of Merv who flourished about A.D. 850, Moses Bar-Kepha his contemporary, Bar-Salibi and Bar-Hebraeus, who belong respectively to the 12th and 13th centuries. And to them must be added Ephrem himself, as a source for the original Syriac of the commentary. For it will be found that he has often incorporated portions of his own hymns, which appear in the Armenian text in the disguise of unsuspected prose[1].

Of the other writers quoted, Isho'dad is a Nestorian, Bar-Kepha and the two later doctors are Monophysites, so that we may say that the whole Syrian church has laid its hands on Ephrem's commentary. The only thing we may have to be careful about will be the handling of cases where Ephrem's language might seem to favour unduly one or other of the great parties in the Syrian church. In such passages the text as transcribed by a learned doctor might easily become suspect.

Of these writers, unfortunately, none is at present in print, except in part Bar-Hebraeus; his commentary on Matthew in the work called the Storehouse of Mysteries was edited by Spanuth in 1879 ; and that on the Gospel of John in 1878 by Schwartz.

---

noted above from Is. li. 1, where Mösinger says, 'quo loco, nescio. The following are some of the corrections to be made.

p. 63, note 4, for *Fortasse ex Is. xlix.* 10 read *Amos viii.* 11.

p. 122, l. 11, for *Marc. i.* 32 read *Jer. xv.* 19.

p. 138, note 1, *where M. refers the reading* 'qui blasphemat Deum, crucifigatur' to *Lev. xxiv.* 16 correct to *Deut. xxi.* 23.

p. 193, for *cf. Is. liv.* 12, *vel Ez. iii.* 9 read *Amos vii.* 8.

p. 210, note 4, for *Cf. Is. liii.* 11 read *Is. lii.* 15.

p. 228 and p. 280, where the words 'Tu dixisti, Mundus per gratiam aedificabitur' are either quoted or implied, make the reference to Ps. lxxxiii. 3, which in English appears as 'I said, Mercy shall be built up for ever.'

I do not wish to criticize Mösinger severely: some of these passages were difficult to identify. Even if his edition is inadequate, he is a great public benefactor to whom we are all deeply indebted.

[1] An instance may be found on p. 28.

For Bar-Ṣalibi we must also turn to the MSS.: for I do not know that any portion of the commentary on the Gospels is in print, over and above the extracts given by Assemani. A large part of the text was however given in English and Latin translations by Dudley Loftus in the two valuable little books which he published at Dublin in 1672 and 1695[1]; and his MS. translations of the remainder into Latin are preserved in the Bodleian Library[2].

For Moses Bar-Kepha I have consulted a fragmentary MS. containing his commentary on Matthew in the British Museum (Cod. Add. 17,274). Wright's description of the MS. I relegate to a note[3]. The importance of Moses Bar-Kepha in this connection lies in the fact that he knows the Ephrem commentary, which he sometimes expressly refers to, and that he imitates it; and further his commentary is one of the principal sources of Bar-Ṣalibi, who expressly names him in his preface as one of the authors whom he has laid under contribution. Anything, therefore, in which the two writers agree, must be read as from the pen of Moses Bar-Kepha, and not from Bar-Ṣalibi. Probably it will be found that Moses, in his turn, derives many of his comments from earlier sources.

---

[1] *The Exposition of Dionysius Syrus*, written above 900 years since, on the Evangelist St Mark, translated by D. L. (Dublin, 1672); *A clear and learned Explication of the History of our Blessed Saviour Jesus Christ*,…by Dionysius Syrus ;… faithfully translated by Dudley Loftus, Dublin, 1695.

[2] *Fell MSS.*, Nos. 6 and 7.

[3] Wright, *Cat. Syr. MSS.*, II. 620. A volume measuring about 14¾ in. by 8¾, made up of portions of several paper MSS. It consists of 260 leaves, a great many of which are more or less torn. The quires are signed with letters. Each page is divided into two columns. Though written by several hands, the character throughout is a good regular cursive of the xith or xiith cent. The contents are as follows:

  (1) Portions of a Commentary upon the Book of Genesis by Moses bar Kiphā…

  (2) Portions of a Commentary on the Gospels, with a long introduction, by Moses bar Kiphā:

    (*a*) Introduction. Fol. 26 *a*.

    (*b*) Commentary on St Matthew. Fol. 50 *a* (should be 48 *a*).

    (*c*) A single fragment of the Commentary on St Luke. Fol. 152 *a*.

  (3) Portions of a Commentary on the Gospel of St Matthew, by some other author. Fol. 121 *a*.

  (4) Portions of a Commentary on the Pauline Epistles by Moses bar Kiphā:

    (*a*) On the Epistle to the Romans. Fol. 153 *a*.

    (*b*) On the First Epistle to the Corinthians. Title, fol. 190 *b*.

    (*c*) On the Second Epistle to the Corinthians. Fol. 239 *a*.

    (*d*) A single fragment of the Commentary on the Epistle to the Galatians.

The proof of Bar-Kepha's acquaintance with the Ephrem commentary is, as we have said, (i) direct, for in discussing the question whether Judas partook of the Eucharist or not, he gives Ephrem's opinion as to the washing off the sanctification of the bread by dipping it in water; and says it is from his Exposition of the Gospel; (ii) there is an indirect proof of his dependence in his imitation of the opening sentences of Ephrem, as will be seen by a reference to our collection of extracts at p. 24. Bar-Kepha also, in his introductory chapters, appears to be the source of Bar-Salibi, and the references to the Diatessaron are, therefore, important for himself and for later writers. It will be found that he carefully distinguishes Tatian's Diatessaron from that of Ammonius.

Amongst the works to which Bar-Kepha refers, there is one which seems to be older than Ephrem, and to have been used by him, and which may perhaps be of great antiquity. The reader of Ephrem will have observed that there is often a strain of interpretation which consists in a very simple allegorisation of the Gospel and its contained parables. Such glosses as (Mös. p. 166) occur in the interpretation of the Planting of the Vineyard,

Colonus = lex,
Tres anni = tempus quo eis ostendit, se esse Salvatorem,

and those which we have quoted from p. 192, seem to belong to a simpler and more archaic hand than that of Ephrem, and they occur in all the commentators.

Bar-Kepha says expressly in one place that these very elementary comments come from a book which he calls

ܗܘܦܟܝܐ ܕܟܬܒܐ ܕܡܬܝ

or the Succinct Exposition of Matthew.

It is, as we have said, quite possible that we have here the traces of some very early document. At all events nothing could be more simple or childlike than the commentary which Bar-Kepha quotes, and to which other commentators evidently allude.

Of Isho'dad nothing has been published beyond a few references by my American friends Dr Hall and Prof. Gottheil; the copy from which I have worked is Cod. Add. 1973 in the Cambridge University Library: and it is from this source that most of my identifications have been made. It is a late paper MS. in the Nestorian character, consisting of 323 leaves; originally there were more, but a number of leaves have disappeared at the beginning of the book, which is a commentary on the Pentateuch, and I think a single leaf has gone at the end. Possibly there may be one or two lacunae. The Gospels begin as follows: Matthew on f. 13 r. (the previous leaves being occupied by the remains of the Commentary on the Pentateuch), Mark on f. 145 v., Luke on f. 169 v., and John on f. 237 r. (ending on f. 323 v.). As might be expected, the Commentary is largely of the nature of Catena, and the authors quoted are sometimes (but not often) indicated by a rubricated name and by a rubric punctuation. The interest of the Commentary lies chiefly in the wealth of unknown or imperfectly known authors whom it quotes: of these the principal are Ephrem and Theodore of Mopsuestia (the latter under the name of 'the Interpreter'); but beyond these, and some of the conventional Greek fathers who were early translated into Syriac, we shall find, Nestorius, Ḥannana (of Ḥedhaiyabh), Babai the Great, Babai the Persian, Honain, and other valuable writers, as well as references to lost books, such as the Diatessaron and the Succinct Exposition of Matthew, which are quoted by title: occasionally he refers to a book of traditions by Hebrew Christians which supplement the Gospel narrative[1]. So valuable is the work that it deserves to be published in full, for it contains almost all that is important in later writers like Bar-Salibi and Bar-Hebraeus, and in an earlier form. I hope to be able to commit it to the press before long, but as my first interest in the work centres in the extracts from Ephrem and from the Diatessaron, I have collected these as far as they have come under my notice in reading, and the result lies in the following pages, supplemented by such parallels and augmentations as I have been able to draw from the great Monophysite Doctors. It is needless to say that no attempt is made at completeness. Not only must there be many passages of the Ephrem commentary extant in Syriac which we have failed to recognize, but it is reasonable to suppose that the Armenian Commentary by the aid of which we make our identifications has often suffered from contraction, in either the

---

[1] For example we are told that Simeon, who carried our Lord in his arms, was the son of Honia, who was the son of Honia a priest, who was the father of Jesus Bar-Sira.

process of translation or the course of tradition, so that portions of
Ephrem may be found in Isho'dad and elsewhere (either expressly
named or recognized by their pronounced Ephremitic flavour)
which we are unable to place in their proper connexion in the
Commentary, or which we can only place there with much hesita-
tion. For passages of this kind a good margin must be left.

Enough has probably been said to shew the importance of the
new Commentary. Attention had already been drawn to it by
two American scholars, first by Dr Isaac H. Hall, who has the
credit of opening the mine, and then by Prof. Gottheil, who had
used some of the direct references to the Diatessaron, which are
contained in it.

Dr Hall's article will be found in the *Journal of Biblical
Literature*, Vol. XI., 1891, Pt 11, pp. 153—155[1], and Prof. Gottheil's in the same periodical, Vol. XII., 1892, Pt 1, pp. 68—71.
It is to these notices that I am indebted for my knowledge of
Isho'dad and his Commentary, and for the suggestions of its bearing upon the Diatessaron and associated questions. That it is
really the work of Isho'dad may be seen:

(i) from the statement of the Nestorian bibliographer 'Ebed-
yeshu or 'Abd-isho' (†1318), who tells us that Isho'dad composed
inter alia an exposition of the New Testament;

(ii) from the headings and subscriptions of the MS., which tell
us clearly that this is the book spoken of by 'Abd-isho'. Thus the
Cambridge copy on f. 13 r. says:

'By the help of the Lord Jesus Christ we begin to write the
Light of the New Testament, which the lover of learning Mar
Isho'dad of Merv[2], bishop of Hedatha[3] in Assyria, toiled over and
collected from the writings of the interpreters and teachers of
the holy Church. Our Lord, help me, and save me, and make
me wise by the grace of thy mercy. Amen.'

On the last leaf we read as follows:

'Here is ended by the help of him who created this world [cod.
adds 'the maker'] this book of the Light of the Gospel which is
full of light which was made by the holy governor Mar Isho'dad
the blessed, bishop of the district of Assyria....'

It will be noticed that there is some confusion in the titles

---

[1] It passed to Germany through a notice of Dr Nestle.

[2] Cod. ܡܪܘܙܝܐ.   [3] Cod. ܚܕܬܐ.

and subscriptions. Isho'dad is called deMaruzaya, where we should have expected Maruzaya or merely deMaru[1]. Further the closing subscription calls him Bishop of the region of Assyria, without naming the city.

But, however this may be, the name of the author is clearly given, and there is no doubt that it is the Nestorian writer of whom 'Abd-isho' speaks, and whom Wright, in his *Syriac Literature* (p. 220), described as follows:

'Isho'dadh of Marū or Merv, bishop of Ḥĕdhattā or al-Hadithah, was a competitor with Theodosius for the patriarchate in 852. According to 'Abhd-isho' his principal work was a Commentary on the New Testament, of which there are MSS. in Berlin, Sachau 311, and in the collection of the S.P.C.K.[2] It extended however to the Old Testament as well, for in Cod. Vat. cccclvii. we find the portions relating to Genesis and Exodus.'

The S.P.C.K. MS. to which Wright alludes is the one which we use from the Cambridge University Library: it contains, as we said above, part of the Commentary on the Pentateuch[3]. There is also a copy (= Bodl. Or. 624) in the Bodleian Library at Oxford.

We shall now give some of the references to the Diatessaron which are found in Isho'dad, after which we shall pass on to collect the fragments which Isho'dad has extracted from Ephrem's Commentary upon the Diatessaron, in connexion with which we shall have to ask whether the acquaintance of the writer with Ephrem extends beyond the commentary in question.

It is very important to observe that the allusions both to the Diatessaron and to the Ephrem Commentary are so extensive that it is necessary to allow that the quotations involve an actual acquaintance with the works in question, and consequently there is no room for doubting Isho'dad's further statement that the Ephrem Commentary is a commentary upon the text of Tatian. It may seem unnecessary to make this last remark, but it is important to remember that the identification has been questioned in certain quarters, and every piece of evidence upon the point is useful.

---

[1] Is there any chance of this being the same person as Isho' Maruzaya or Isho' of Merv, the compiler of a Syriac lexicon, which was one of the sources of Bar 'Ali's glosses? see Wright, *Syriac Literature*, p. 215.

[2] i.e. the Society for the Promotion of Christian Knowledge.

[3] Three other MSS. are said to exist in America, viz. two in the Library of Lane Theological Seminary, one (incomplete) in the possession of Dr Hall.

But when we say that Ephrem commented upon the text of the Diatessaron, we do not mean to imply that the text of the Diatessaron had come down unchanged to Ephrem's day. It had two hundred years of life before it reached Ephrem's hands, and, loyal as Syria was to her great teacher and evangelist, we have no right to suppose that the Diatessaron enjoyed an immunity from correction of which the Gospels in their separate form shew no signs. If they were corrected again and again, the Diatessaron was not likely to escape from similar treatment. It need not have been reformed to the Peshito in Ephrem's time, and the evidence is clear that it was not; but the evidence is also clear that in passages which were of dogmatic importance, as well as in some of a less pronounced character, the hand of the corrector was laid upon the text. The same thing happened after Ephrem had done his work, for, as we have seen, the Commentary will often shew earlier readings than the text. More than that, an adventurous writer has occasionally aired his own erudition on Ephrem's pages by telling us what the Greek text is, and sometimes has displaced the original Syriac by his obtrusive activity[1].

Let us then examine into the direct traces of the Diatessaron in Isho'dad.

1. In the prologue to Mark (f. 146 r.) we are told

i.e. Titianos the disciple of Justin the philosopher and martyr selected from the four gospels and combined and composed a Gospel and called it Diatessaron, i.e. of the Combined; and on the Divinity of Christ he did not write; and upon this Gospel Mar Ephrem commented.

[The extract is given by Gottheil, l. c. p. 70.]

This statement reappears with slight changes, some amplification, and not a little ultimate confusion, in Bar-Salibi and in Bar-Hebraeus. Bar-Salibi does not have the sentence 'and on the

---

[1] It will be seen that I am now satisfied that the references to the 'Graecus' in the Commentary are not from Ephrem, but some later person.

Divinity of Christ he did not write,' nor does Bar-Hebraeus. Both of them add that the combined Gospel begins with the words 'In the beginning was the Word.' Both of them change ܚܠܛ ܘܚܒܫ of Isho'dad into ܚܒܛ ܘܚܒܫ, which suggests the dependence of Bar-Hebraeus on Bar-Ṣalibi. The word ܚܠܛ is justified by the following ܚܘܠܛܐ. Finally, Bar-Hebraeus combines with the whole passage (if indeed he is the first to do so) the language of Eusebius with regard to the Diatessaron of Ammonius[1].

2. In discussing the opening verses of S. Mark's Gospel, Isho'dad distinguishes the reading of the Diatessaron of Tatian from that of Ammonius[2].

f. 149 r.

ܐܚܪ̈ܢܐ. ܕܟܬܒܐ ܠܗ ܕܕܝܛܣܪܘܢ ܕܚܒܫ ܒܐܠܟܣܢܕܪܝܐ
ܚܠܦ ܗܝ ܕܕܝܐܛܣܪܘܢ ܕܟܬܝܒ ܒܐܫܥܝܐ ܒܢܒ̈ܝܐ ܐܡܪ

i.e. Others say: that the book of the Diatessaron which was composed[3] in Alexandria says instead of the passage of the Diatessaron 'it is written in Isaiah,' '[it is written] in the prophets.'

Here the distinction is clearly drawn between the two Diatessarons and it is affirmed that Tatian read ἐν Ἠσαΐᾳ and Ammonius ἐν τοῖς προφήταις. It may be questioned, Does not this involve the admission that Tatian began his Gospel with Mark? The answer, however, must be in the negative. What the commentator has referred to in Tatian is not Mark, but Matthew (iii. 3), as may be seen by comparing the words ascribed to Tatian

ܕܟܬܝܒ ܒܐܫܥܝܐ

with the Old Syriac translation of ὁ ῥηθεὶς διὰ Ἠσαΐου in Matt. iii. 3.

ܕܟܬܝܒ. ܥܠܘܗܝ ܒܐܫܥܝܐ

[1] Note that the same statements are made again in Bar-Ṣalibi's preface to the four Gospels, which Loftus does into Latin as follows:

c. 33. Nonnulli dicunt quod Eusebius Caesariensis quando observasset Eumonium Alexandrinum confecisse Evangelium διατέσσαρον (sic!) vocatum (hoc est) e quatuor, et adhaerentiam verborum mutasse, similiter etiam fecisse Titianum Graecum haereticum, ipse coegit (l. collegit) illa quatuor et eorum singula seorsim scripsit.

[2] This passage was wrongly translated by me in the *Contemporary Review* (Aug. 1895).

[3] lege ܕܚܒܝܫ ܗܘܐ *which was composed.*

The reference, therefore, to Mark in Tatian is a misunderstanding. As to the reference to Ammonius, this is probably correct, for there is reason to believe that in Ammonius the Gospels are kept distinct.

As we have said, Isho'dad carefully distinguishes the two Diatessarons; it is otherwise with his followers, to whom the confusion was natural enough: and in one place of Bar-Ṣalibi which deals with this very passage before us the confusion is obvious, though it may be questioned whether it may not be due to faulty transcription, since Bar-Ṣalibi elsewhere makes the distinction clearly enough. At all events, here is the passage, with the accompanying translation of Loftus.

ܐܚܪ̈ܢܐ. ܕܒܟܬܒܐ ܕܕܝܐܛܣܪܘܢ ܕܢܛܝܪ ܒܐܠܟܣܢܕܪܝܐ
ܕܟܬܝܒ ܠܛܛܝܐܢܘܣ ܐܦܝܣܩܘܦܐ. ܘܐܦ ܒܐܘܢܓܠܝܘܢ
ܝܘܢܝܐ ܘܚܪܩܠܝܐ. ܒܢܒܝܐ ܟܬܝܒ ܟܕ ܠܐ ܡܦܪܫ
ܕܡܢܘ ܢܒܝܐ

'Others [say] that in the book of Diatessaron which is preserved[1] in Alexandria and was written by Tatianus the Bishop, as also in the Greek Gospel and in the Harkalian, it is written "In the prophet," without explaining what prophet.'

The exact genesis of the confusion is not easily determined; the passage evidently leans on early statements as to the composition of the Diatessaron of Ammonius; and it is quite possible that it is merely a blundering restatement of the passage given above from Isho'dad, with the name of the author of the better-known Diatessaron brought in from a marginal gloss.

3. (f. 29 r.) On Matt. i. 20 Isho'dad remarks, *inter alia*,

ܐܚܪ̈ܢܐ. ܕܗܘ ܠܡ ܕܦܫܩ ܡܢ ܥܒܪܝܐ ܠܣܘܪܝܝܐ
ܫܚܠܦ ܡܠܬܐ ܘܚܠܦ ܗܝ ܕܐܬܒܛܢ ܒܗ̇ ܗܘ ܕܐܬܝܠܕ.
ܕܛܛܝܢܘܣ[2] ܐܡܪ ܕܝܢ. ܕܗܘ ܠܡ ܕܐܬܝܠܕ ܒܗ̇. ܡܢ
ܪܘܚܐ ܗܘ ܕܩܘܕܫܐ.

'Others say: that the one who translated from Hebrew into Syriac changed the word, and instead of the expression "that

[1] Or *composed*. [2] Cod. ܕܛܛܝܢܗ (sic).

which is begotten in her," used the words "that which is born in her;" but the Diatessaron says "that which is born in her, is from the Holy Ghost."' [The extract is given by Gottheil, l. c. p. 69.]

4. On Matt. iii. 5, according to Isho'dad[1],

ܕܝܛܣܪܘܢ ܕܝܢ ܐܡܪ. ܡܐܟܘܠܬܗ ܠܗ ܕܒܫܐ
ܘܚܠܒܐ ܕܛܘܪܐ

i.e. The Diatessaron says, His meat was honey and milk of the mountains.

We correct the text to 'milk and honey of the mountains,' and remark that 'of the mountains' is the translation of *ἄγριος*: [cf. Cod. Ludov. *in loc.*, and the Palestine Syriac version *passim*].

As this passage influences both Bar-Ṣalibi and Bar-Hebraeus, I give the remainder of Dr Hall's extract for the sake of comparison.

'But the Diatessaron says, His food indeed was honey and milk of the mountains. Others, the locusts indeed are tender roots that resemble parsnep, i.e. *gezar*, and not very pleasant to the taste: which some call *qamšis* but others *qamšin*, but in Persian *mang*. Others say that they are roots which are called *qauche*, which in form indeed is like locusts, but in taste sweet, like honey. Others that they are shoots of plants, and also that this is what is meant by the honey. This is not sweet they say, but that is bitter and loathsome which wild bees make[2].

According to the Expositor, locusts are winged creatures, and the honey is that of nature; that is from the warmth of place [i.e. its habitat is warm] and its constitution air, since it is continually found there [lit. they continually find it there].'

The corresponding passage in Bar-Ṣalibi is as follows:

ܐܚܪ̈ܢܐ. ܕܒܕܝܛܣܪܘܢ ܐܘܢܓܠܝܘܢ ܕܐܪܒܥܐ ܟܬܝܒ
ܕܡܐܟܘܠܬܗ ܚܠܒܐ ܘܕܒܫܐ ܕܒܪܐ: ܟܕ ܚܠܒܐ ܚܫܚ
ܗܘܐ ܠܛܠܝܘܬܗ ܘܕܒܫܐ ܠܓܒܪܘܬܐ ܠܓܢܒܪܘܬܐ

i.e. Others say: that in the Diatessaron, i.e. the Gospel of Four, it is written that his meat was milk and honey of the wild[3]; since milk was proper to his youth and honey to the manly age[4].

[1] The Cambridge copy has been somewhat abbreviated at this point. I follow Dr Hall's text.

[2] This betrays the hand of a person who lived in Armenia, whose bitter honey has been spoken of by Xenophon and later travellers.

[3] Note the correction of the primitive reading.

[4] Cod. Mus. Brit. Add. 12,143, fol. 52.

Finally, we have in Bar-Hebraeus: "His meat was locusts and honey of the wild....Some say that 'locusts' means roots and sweet plants (*qauche*), but in the Diatessaron 'milk and honey' is written."

It is interesting to study these passages and note the influence of the primitive Encratite reading, and of allied alternative readings. Tatian substituted 'milk' for 'locusts'; and one might naturally ask how he found a supply of this aliment in the wilderness. The answer is in Bar-Ṣalibi; he was taken into the wilderness by his mother, who *for fifteen years* ministered to his needs[1]. But there were other vegetarian readings besides that of Tatian; we see traces of them in the language of Isho'dad; precisely as the Gospel according to the Hebrews had substituted for ἀκρίδες the similarly sounding ἐγκρίδες, some Syrian reformers had found a vegetable word ܡܕܚܡ which sounded very nearly like ܩܡܨܐ. We can thus get some measure of the extent of the hostility to the 'locusts' among early believers. They were great lovers of clean provender.

A further curious instance of the hostility of the Eastern Christians to the locusts in the diet of St John the Baptist has been pointed out to me by Prof. Nestle. It occurs in a story told to Peter the Iberian by Peter the disciple of Abba Isaia, to the effect that when his teacher was sick and near to death, he was overheard to be in conversation with some unknown person; and a subsequent enquiry on the part of the disciple elicited the information that the mysterious person addressed was St John the Baptist, who had answered the question as to what were the locusts that he had eaten in the wilderness, in the following words:

ܕܠܒܘܬܐ ܕܥܩܪܐ ܕܒܪܐ ܐܝܬܝܗܘܢ ܗܘܘ.

"They were the hearts [*or* pith] of wild roots." See Payne Smith, Col. 3649 s.v. ܩܡܨܐ.

5. It was suspected by Zahn from the Commentary of Ephrem on the Baptism of our Lord, that there stood in his text some allusion to the fire at the Jordan and the light which blazed forth when Christ was baptized. As the text, however, is non-extant in this part of the Commentary, it might be thought that this conjecture of Zahn's was somewhat hazardous. Why, it may

---

[1] Porphyry is credited with a somewhat similar experience.

be said, may not Ephrem have known the tradition from other sources than Tatian?

But Zahn is justified by the extract from Isho'dad (f. 43 v.) which we have printed on p. 43, in which it is expressly stated, according to the Diatessaron, that 'light shined forth at the Jordan.'

6. The next passage tells us of a curious primitive rendering of the word συκομορέα in the Diatessaron, which, as we shall see, was not in Ephrem's copy.

f. 100 v.

[Syriac text, five lines]

i.e. Others say: that Bethphage means the place of insipid figs: and they bring forward testimony from the Diatessaron and the Greek version; in the story that little Zachaeus, who was little of stature and little of soul, climbed up into the Phagē that he might see Jesus; and this is in Syriac called the insipid fig-tree. [Cf. Bar-Bahlul who says that this Phagē is the reading of the Combined Gospel.]

Here then we have the translation of 'sycomore' by Tatian; and now turn to Ephrem *in loc.* (Mösinger, p. 180) and we shall find him calling it a 'surda ficulnea,' and making comments upon Zacchaeus, who was not to remain '*in surditate.*' Is this an interpretation of *[Syriac]*, or is it not an intermediate stage in which the text has been corrected to *[Syriac]*?

If this is not the explanation, what are we to say of Ephrem's *surdus?*

It appears, then, that we have recovered a number of passages in which the reading of the Diatessaron is expressly given by Isho'dad.

But there is also more light to be obtained from the later commentators who, though they appear to depend upon Isho'dad in the information which they furnish, do not wholly depend upon him. For example, there is a very important passage in which Bar-Ṣalibi seems to intimate that Tatian gave no harmonized account of the Resurrection. Every reader of Ephrem's text as current in the Armenian will have been struck by the poverty of the Commentary at this part of the Gospel; and no doubt suspicions will have arisen that there was something 'uncanny' in the text of Tatian where the Resurrection is recorded.

Now Bar-Ṣalibi expressly says[1], in the prologue to the Gospels, c. 33:

ܐܘܣܒܝܘܣ ܩܣܪܝܐ ܐܬܒܛܠ ܠܗ ܕܢܣܝܡ ܠܩܢܘܢܐ
ܕܐܘܢܓܠܝܘܢ. ܘܝܕܝܥܐ ܗܕܐ ܡܢ ܐܓܪܬܗ ܕܠܘܬ
ܩܪܦܝܢܘܣ. ܘܢܚܘܐ ܒܗܘܢ ܫܘܝܘܬܐ ܕܐܘܢܓܠܣܛܐ.
ܟܬܒ ܗܘܐ ܐܡܘܢܝܘܣ ܐܦ ܛܛܝܐܢܘܣ ܐܘܢܓܠܝܘܢ
ܕܝܛܣܪܘܢ ܐܘܟܝܬ ܕܐܪܒܥ. ܐܝܟܢܐ ܕܐܡܪܢ ܡܢ
ܠܥܠ. ܘܟܕ ܐܬܘ ܠܘܬ ܬܫܥܝܬܐ ܕܩܝܡܬܐ ܘܚܙܘ
ܕܫܘܚܠܦܐ ܫܒܩܘ ܠܫܘܠܡܗܘܢ. ܘܐܘܣܒܝܘܣ ܐܬܒܛܠ
ܠܗ ܕܢܥܒܕ ܠܗܠܝܢ ܩܢܘܢܐ ܘܒܗܘܢ ܢܚܘܐ ܟܠ
ܫܠܡܘܬܗܘܢ ܕܐܘܢܓܠܣܛܐ...

a passage which Loftus does into Latin as follows:

'Eusebius Caesariensis sollicitus fuit ut constitueret Canones Evangelii quod constat ex Epistola ejus ad Carpianum, et in iis monstret harmoniam Evangelistarum. Scripserant enim Eumonius et Titianus etiam Evangelium vocatum διατέσσαρον [sic] (i.e.) quatuor prout supra diximus, et quando venerant ad historiam resurrectionis et observaverant variationem abstinuerunt ab ipsa opera, sed Eusebio curae erat, ut hujusmodi Canones conficeret, et ostenderet Evangelistarum inter se convenientiam...'

Here we are expressly told that Tatian and Ammonius found it impossible to harmonize the Gospels of the Resurrection and gave up the attempt. Whatever may be the meaning of this, it is an important passage, and needs to be carefully weighed by those who like myself have been arguing freely from the contents and arrangement of the Arabic Harmony in its closing chapters.

Moses Bar-Kepha, as we have said, appears to be connected with the source of some of the disputable matter in Bar-Ṣalibi and Bar-Hebraeus. For this reason I transcribe the sentences in which Moses speaks of Eusebius and his Canons. In his introductory chapters we have as follows:

[1] Cod. Mus. Brit. 12,143.

c. 53.

i.e. c. 53, Which shews who collected the four books of the Evangelists and set them in order in one book.

And some people, indeed, say that Eusebius of Cesarea, when he saw that Julianus (sic! for Ammonius) of Alexandria made the Gospel of the Diatessaron, i.e. by means of Four, and changed the sequence of things in the Gospels, and that Tatian also the Greek, the heretic leader, made a Gospel which is called Tasaron (sic!) and he too changed the sequence of things; he, Eusebius, took care and collected the four books of the four Evangelists and set them in order and placed them in one book, and preserved the body of their compositions as it was without taking anything from them or adding anything to them, and made certain Canons on account of their harmony one with another.

A very similar account will be found on f. 40 v., where Bar-Kepha discusses the Canons of Eusebius. In neither passage is there the slightest sign of any confusion between Tatian and Ammonius.

We now pass to another point upon which a few words must be said: viz. the extent of Isho'dad's acquaintance with the writings of Ephrem. A mere superficial glance at the extracts

---

[1] The MS. is torn; we restore from the parallel passages.

which we have identified will suffice to shew that he was a close and careful reader of the Ephrem Commentary. Did he extract from any other parts of Ephrem's works? The answer is affirmative; for example, in commenting on Matt. xxvi. 29 (f. 127 v.) he says

ܘܐܦ ܡܪܝ ܐܦܪܝܡ ܒܡܐܡܪܐ ܕܥܠ ܒܝܬ ܕܢܚܐ.
ܡܢ ܠܚܡܐ ܠܡ ܕܚܝܐ ܕܐܬܝܗܒ ܠܥܠܡܐ. ܠܐ ܠܡܠܐܟܐ
ܐܟܠܘ ܐܠܐ ܡܪܗܘܢ ܕܡܠܐܟܐ. ܡܢ ܗܘ ܓܝܪ ܠܚܡܐ
ܕܐܟܠ ܠܡ ܬܠܡܝܕܘܗܝ ܡܟܐ ܘܠܗܠ.

i.e. And Mar Ephrem also in his discourse on the Epiphany [says], 'Of the bread of life that is given to the world, it was not the angels that they ate, but the Lord of the angels' &c.

I have not, however, identified the passage in the printed works of Ephrem.

There are a number of passages which are more difficult to assign to their sources: we give a selection from them by way of illustration.

Matt. iii. 4 (f. 39 r.)

ܡܪܝ ܐܦܪܝܡ ܘܐܚܪܢܐ ܐܡܪܝܢ. ܕܐܠܝܫܒܥ ܫܢܬܗ
ܡܢ ܣܝܦܗ ܕܗܪܘܕܣ. ܩܒܠܬ ܠܡ ܓܠܝܢܐ ܕܬܥܪܘܩܝܘܗܝ
ܠܡܕܒܪܐ. ܟܕ ܥܒܕܬ ܠܗ ܡܢ ܚܟܡܬܐ ܦܝܣܢܝܬܐ
ܟܘܬܝܢܐ ܕܣܥܪܐ ܕܥܡܪܐ ܕܓܡܠܐ. ܡܪܝ ܐܦܪܝܡ
ܒܠܚܘܕ ܩܪܐ ܥܡܪܐ. ܥܡܪܐ ܕܣܥܪܐ ܕܥܠ ܟܪܣܗ
ܕܓܡܠܐ. ܕܠܐ ܩܫܐ ܛܒ.

i.e. Mar Ephrem and others say that Elisabeth withdrew him from the sword of Herod; she received, indeed, a revelation to run away with him to the wilderness; while she made him from kind forethought (lit. gracious wisdom) a coat of hair of the wool of camels. Mar Ephrem only reads wool; the wool of the hair which is on the belly of camels which is not very rough.

Bar-Ṣalibi has access to similar traditions when he says (Loftus, p. 83), "The Lord Ephraim saith, That she received direction by vision, to fly from the sword of Herod, and that she made him a coat of camel's hair and a girdle to bind his loyns."

Luke iii. 19 (f. 78 r.)

ܡܪܝ ܐܦܪܝܡ ܘܐܚܪ̈ܢܐ ܐܡܪܝܢ ܕܒܬܪ ܡܘܬܗ
ܕܦܝܠܝܦܘܣ ܢܣܒܗ̇

Mar Ephrem and others say that Herod took her [Herodias] after the death of Philip.

Luke iv. 26 (f. 14 r.)

[ܐܠܐ] ܐܚܝ ܠܒܪܗ̇ ܕܐܪܡܠܬܐ ܨܪܦܬܝܬܐ. ܗܢܘ
ܕܝܢ ܐܝܬܘܗܝ ܗܘܐ ܝܘܢܐ. ܐܝܟ ܣܗܕܘܬܐ ܕܥܒܪ̈ܝܐ
ܘܕܡܪܝ ܐܦܪܝܡ

i.e. Elias raised up the son of the widow of Sarepta; and this was Jonah, according to the testimony of the Hebrews and of Mar Ephrem.

Matt. xxvi. 75 (f. 132 r.)

ܡܪܝ ܐܦܪܝܡ ܕܝܢ ܠܗܠܝܢ ܕܬܪܬܝܢ ܙܒܢܝܢ ܥܠ
ܫܘܢܝܬܐ ܕܩܪܝܗ ܕܬܪܢܓܠܐ ܣܡ ܠܗ ܕܩܪܐ ܠܡ
ܘܐܪܟܬܗ̇ ܐܚܕ ܒܐܚܪܬܐ ܐܝܟ ܕܩܪܝܬܐ ܥܠ ܩܪܝܬܐ
ܬܗܘܐ. ܐܝܟ ܕܠܣܗܕܘܬܐ ܝܬܝܪܬܐ ܕܥܠ ܫܡܥܘܢ

i.e. But Mar Ephrem refers these two times [of cock-crowing] to the repetition of the crowing of the cock; which crowed and immediately continued with another crow, that there might be crow upon crow, with a view to the greater testimony to Simon.

Matt. xxvii. 19 (f. 133 v.)

ܡܪܝ ܐܦܪܝܡ ܕܝܢ ܕܒܡܕܒܪܢܘܬܐ ܠܡ ܐܠܗܝܬܐ
ܛܥܬܗ ܠܚܠܡܗ̇ ܘܠܐ ܐܫܬܥܝܬ ܠܗ ܟܕ ܐܝܬܘܗܝ
ܒܒܝܬܐ ܐܝܟܢܐ ܕܟܕ ܫܠܚܐ ܠܗ ܠܒܝܬ ܕܝܢܐ ܒܬܪ
ܕܐܬܬ ܠܥܘܗܕܢܗ̇ ܒܬܗܪܐ ܢܦܠ ܟܠܢܫ

[The question is, why did not Pilate's wife tell him her dream in the night?] Mar Ephrem says that by Divine providence she forgot her dream and did not tell him when he was in the house, in order that when she sends to him to the judgment hall, after it has come to her remembrance, everyone may fall into astonishment.

EXTRACTS FROM THE COMMENTARY OF EPHREM ON THE GOSPEL.

Mösinger, p. 1.

John i. 1. Quare Dominus noster carnem induit? Ut ipsa caro victoriae gaudia gustaret, et dona gratiae explorata et cognita haberet. Si Deus sine carne vicisset, quae ei tribuerentur laudes?

Imitated by Moses Bar-Kepha (f. 27, a. 2).

ܐܢ ܓܝܪ ܐܠܗܐ ܙܟܐ
ܠܣܛܢܐ ܕܠܐ ܦܓܪܐ ܐܝܢܐ
ܬܫܒܘܚܬܐ ܗܘܐ ܠܦܓܪܐ.
ܐܠܐ ܐܬܚܝܕ ܠܒܣܪܐ
ܘܠܢܦܫܐ ܐܝܟܢܐ ܕܦܓܪܐ
ܕܚܒ . . . ܢܙܟܐ ܠܣܛܢܐ

i.e. For if God conquered Satan without a body, what glory is it to the body? But he was united to flesh and soul that the body which was the debtor...might overcome Satan.

Cf. also (f. 27, a. 1).

ܡܛܠ ܗܕܐ ܐܬܒܣܪ
ܐܝܟܢܐ ܕܢܬܘܬܦ ܒܛܒܘܬܗ
ܟܡܐ ܕܡܟܢܐ

On this account he was incarnate that it (the body) might participate in his goodness, as far as it is possible.

Bar-Kepha begins his commentary with a long chapter on the reasons why our Lord became incarnate, the heading being

c. 1. Sheweth the reasons on account of which God the Word was incarnate and became man.

He evidently follows Ephrem at the very opening of his book, though he does not name his model.

Mösinger, p. 6.

Hoc verbum caro factum est et habitavit in vobis.

Probably preserved in Isho'dad (f. 297 r.).

ܘܐܠܘ ܐܡܪ ܦܓܪܐ
ܡܣܬܒܪ ܗܘܐ ܕܦܓܪܐ
ܐܚܬ ܡܢ ܫܡܝܐ. ܘܟܢ
ܐܫܬܚܠܦ ܠܒܣܪܐ

i.e. And if he had said *body*, it would have been supposed that he had sent down a body from heaven: for this reason it was changed to 'flesh.'

I suspect that something has dropped here from the text of Ephrem, which is represented in the accompanying extract of Isho'dad: as I have suggested on p. 4 it was one of Ephrem's doctrinal points that one should not say that the body of Christ descended from heaven. The trouble occurs again in Isho'dad in connexion with the Old Syriac reading in John vi. 51 'I am the living bread *that descended*,' 'the bread that I will give is my *body*' (so Cod. Ludov., Cod. Curet., and the Palestine text).

Accordingly Isho'dad says[1], He did not wish to teach us that his body was from heaven. It was not the body that descended from heaven, but the power that made the bread a body from heaven, for our Lord was teaching here, not of his own body, but of the bread of the mystery.

ܠܘ ܦܓܪܗ ܡܢ ܫܡܝܐ ܢܠܦ ܕܝܠܗ. ܐܠܐ ܕܚܝܠܐ
ܗܘ ܕܥܒܕ ܠܗ ܠܠܚܡܐ ܦܓܪܐ ܡܢ ܫܡܝܐ ܗܘ. ܥܠ
ܠܚܡܐ ܓܝܪ ܕܐܪܙܐ ܐܠܦ ܡܪܢ ܬܡܢ.

Mösinger, p. 12.

Scripserunt digiti in tabula, 'Joannes,' quod nomen indicat nos misericordia indigere.

Cf. Isho'dad (f. 178 r.).

ܝܘܚܢܢ ܕܝܢ ܚܢܢܐ ܕܐܠܗܐ
ܡܬܦܫܩ.

'John' is interpreted to mean 'the grace of God.'

[1] MS. Univ. Cant. Add. 1973, f. 266 v.

Mösinger, p. 14.

Luke i. 24. Et quod dicit: *Abscondit se Elisabeth*, scilicet ex tristitia de eis quae Zachariae[1] acciderant. Rursus *abscondit se*, quia eam pudebat se decrepitam ad usum matrimoniae rediisse.

Isho'dad (f. 172 r.).

ܗܝ ܕܛܫܝܐ ܢܦܫܗ̇
ܝܪ̈ܚܐ ܚܡܫܐ. ܚܕܐ ܟܕ
ܬܡܝܗܐ ܒܚܕܬܘܬܗ̇ ܕܗܝ
ܕܐܣܬܥܪܬ. ܕܬܪ̈ܬܝܢ.
ܡܛܠ ܟܪܝܘܬܗ ܕܙܟܪܝܐ.
ܘܕܬܠܬ ܡܛܠ ܒܘܣܪܐ
ܕܣܝܒܘܬܗ̇. ܘܕܐܪܒܥ ܡܛܠ
ܕܠܐ ܟܒܪ ܡܫܪܪܐ ܗܘܬ
ܕܡܛܝܐ ܠܡܐܠܕ ܀

i.e. She hid herself five months: (i) because she was astonished at the novelty of what had taken place; (ii) on account of the sorrow of Zacharias; (iii) because of the shame on account of her old age; and (iv) because perhaps she was not sure that she was going to bring forth.

Mösinger, p. 15.

Luke i. 24. De Elisabeth autem scriptum est, *quod se absconderit quinque menses*, donec scilicet membra filii sui formarentur, ut laetabundus coram Domino suo exultaret, et quia Mariae annunciatio prope erat.

The same opinion is repeated on p. 19 in nearly the same words: Ac propterea per sex menses, donec membra infantis perfecta essent, conceptus Elisabeth abscondebatur Mariae, ut infans ante Dominum suum laetabundus exiliret et exiliendo Mariae testis fieret.

Isho'dad (f. 172 v.).

ܕܚܡܫ. ܗܝ ܕܚܬܝܪ
ܚܬܝܬܐ. ܟܕ ܡܫܬܡܠܐ
ܥܘܠܐ ܒܗܕܡܘܗܝ ܠܡܕܘܨ
ܠܩܕܡ ܡܪܗ. ܘܡܛܠ
ܕܣܒܪܬܐ ܐܦ ܡܪܝܡ
ܕܬܬܣܒܪ.

i.e. Fifthly, which is more exact, [she hides herself] while the babe is being perfected in his limbs to exult before his Lord; and because the annunciation is about to be made to Mary also.

[1] M. notes as follows: ad verbum, ex tristitia Zachariae. Non dubito, genitivum objecti hoc loco adesse. The observation is exactly confirmed by the Syriac text, which shews us how literally the Armenian translator had followed his copy.

Mösinger, p. 15.

Luke i. 26. *Mense sexto:* numerat enim Evangelista tempus, ex quo Elisabeth concepit.

Isho'dad (f. 172 v.).

ܗܘ ܕܝܢ ܕܒܝܪܚܐ ܕܫܬܐ
ܐܫܬܠܚ ܡܠܐܟܐ ܠܓܒܪܐܝܠ
ܡܢ ܒܥܣܪܬܐ ܕܬܫܪܝܢ
ܩܕܝܡ.

i.e. In the sixth month the angel Gabriel was sent, reckoned from the tenth day of the former Teshri.

The Armenian text seems here to have abbreviated both the text and comment of Ephrem; for the parallel passage in Isho'dad tells us that the annunciation to Zacharias was made in the sixth month, reckoned from the tenth of the former Teshri. And we find by reference to Mösinger, p. 18 (v. infra), that this is the actual date assigned by Ephrem to the visit of the angel to Zacharias.

Mösinger, p. 16.

Alio loco eadem Scriptura dixit, utrumque, Josephum et Mariam, esse ex domo David.
(Cf. Cod. Ludov. in Luc. ii. 4.)

Cf. Isho'dad (f. 173 r.).

ܗܘ ܕܝܢ ܕܡܢ ܒܝܬܗ
ܕܕܘܝܕ ܠܓܘܢܝܬܐ ܗܘ
ܕܝܘܣܦ ܘܕܒܬܘܠܬܐ.

i.e. The expression 'of the house of David' is common to both Joseph and the Virgin.

Mösinger, p. 17.

Luke i. 39. *Et surgens abiit Maria ad Elisabeth*, ut disceret, num revera ita ei factum esset, et ut, de hoc certior facta, de eo quod ad se spectabat non dubitaret.

Isho'dad (f. 177 r.).

ܗܘ ܕܩܡܬ ܕܝܢ ܡܪܝܡ
ܘܐܙܠܬ ܒܨܝܦܐܝܬ. ܗ̄. ܐܝܟ
ܕܬܒܩܐ ܢܣܝܢܐ ܕܡܢ ܡܠܐܟܐ
ܐܬܡܠܠ ܕܥܠܝܗ̇.

i.e. *Mary rose and went anxiously*, in order that she might make trial of what had been said by the angel concerning her.

Mösinger, p. 18.

Luke i. Post tres autem menses in domum suam reversa est hac ex causa, ne Dominus ante servum suum quasi famulus staret.

Isho'dad (f. 177 v.).

ܒܪܡ ܐܙܠܐ ܒܕܠܐ ܦܐܝܐ
ܗܘܬ ܕܐܡܗ ܕܡܪܢ ܐܡܗ
ܕܥܒܕܐ ܬܫܡܫ.

But she goes home, on account of its not being proper that the mother of our Lord should wait upon the mother of the servant.

Mösinger, p. 18.

Concepit Elisabeth mense Sahmi, postquam Zacharias dies ministerii et officii sui complevit. Annunciatio Mariae evenit decimo die mensis Arek, sicut illa Zachariae decimo die mensis Hori.

Isho'dad (f. 172 v.).

ܐܣܬܒܪ ܕܝܢ ܠܙܟܪܝܐ
ܒܥܣܪܬܐ ܒܬܫܪܝܢ ܩܕܡ.
ܐܣܬܒܪܬ ܕܝܢ ܡܪܝܡ
ܒܥܣܪܬܐ ܒܢܝܣܢ.

i.e. The annunciation was made to Zacharias in the tenth day of the former Teshrin; and to Mary on the tenth day of Nisan.

The translator has given us Hori as the equivalent of the former Teshrin, and Sahmi for the latter Teshrin; Arek stands for Nisan. The latter identification explains the allusion to the flower of Arek on p. 17: by which term either John the Baptist or Christ (it is not quite clear which) is described.

The allusion to the flowery Nisan is exactly in Ephrem's manner; for example *Hymnus de Crucifixione* (Lamy, i. 708):

ܢܝܣܢ ܡܢ ܦܩܥܘ̈ܗܝ
ܟܠܝܠܐ ܢܓܕܠ ܠܗ:

i.e. Let Nisan adorn him with a crown of its flowers;

or *Hymnus de Resurrectione* (Lamy, ii. 762):

ܒܢܝܣܢ ܦܬ̈ܚܝܢ ܠܟܣ̈ܝܗܘܢ
ܦܩ̈ܥܐ ܘܢܦܩܝܢ ܘܘܪ̈ܕܝܗܘܢ

i.e. In Nisan the flowers break open their cups, and their roses blow;

and so *passim*. Cf. ed. Rom. iii. 603, 604 etc.

But, in fact, as will be seen later on, a large piece of this very hymn, beginning with the two lines which we have quoted, is transferred bodily into the Commentary: see under Mösinger, p. 237.

The hymn last quoted explains also why Ephrem says (p. 18) that in the month of Nisan the nakedness of Adam was covered: "eodem die agnus verus in utero virginis inclusus est, quo tempore lux potitur imperio, et per hoc docuit, se venisse, ut Adami nuditatem obtegeret." We may compare (Lamy, ii. p. 763):

ܙܟܐ ܢܝܣܢ ܒܣܝܡܐ.
ܡܡܙܓ ܠܐܐܪ ܒܒܣܝܡܘܬܗ.
ܠܐܝܠܢ̈ܐ ܥܪܛ̈ܠܝܐ ܡܠܒܫ.
ܕܐܪܙܗ ܗܘ ܕܐܒܐ ܕܝܬ̈ܡܐ.
ܦܪܘܣܝܐ ܕܐܪܥܐ ܡܒܗܬ.
ܐܝܟ ܡܪܗ ܕܒܗܬ ܘܐܠܒܫ.
ܦܪܘܣܝܐ ܕܚܘܐ ܒܥܕܢ.

i.e. Sweet Nisan has conquered,
And mingles its sweetness with the air;
It clothes the bare trees,
Which is a mystery of the Father of Orphans;
It shames the nakedness of the earth,
Just as its Lord shamed and clad
The nakedness of Eve in Eden—

or p. 769:

ܗܐ ܬܘܒ ܢܝܣܢ ܠܐܪܥܐ
ܙܩܪ ܡܠܒܫ ܠܗ ܠܒܘܫܐ ܕܟܠ ܓܘ̈ܢܝܢ
ܡܬܥܛܦܐ ܒܪܝܬܐ ܗܘ ܢܚܬܐ ܕܦܩܪ̈ܐ
ܘܦܪܘܣܝܐ ܕܗܒܒ̈ܐ
ܐܡܗ ܕܐܕܡ ܒܥܐܕܐ ܕܢܝܣܢ
ܡܬܥܛܦܐ ܢܚܬܐ ܕܠܐ ܙܩܝܪ ܒܐܝ̈ܕܝܐ

etc.

i.e. Lo, once again Nisan for the earth
Weaves and clothes her with a garb of all hues;
The creation is clad with a robe of flowers
And a tunic of blossoms.
The mother of Adam in the feast of Nisan
Is clad with a robe not woven of hands.

Mösinger, p. 21.

Id propter seriem regum factum est, quia impossibile erat, ut infans nomine matris suae genealogiae inscriberetur, hac autem ratione filius David regibus adscriptus est.

cf. Ephrem (ed. Rom. iii. 601).

ܫܘܒܠ ܡܠܟ̈ܐ ܚܠܦ ܢܫ̈ܐ
ܒܫܡ ܓܒܪ̈ܐ ܗܘ ܐܬܟܬܒ.
ܝܘܣܦ ܒܪ ܕܘܝܕ ܡܟܝܪܗ̇
ܠܒܪܬ ܕܘܝܕ. ܕܠܐ ܡܫܟܚ
ܛܠܝܐ ܕܢܬܟܬܒ ܒܫܡ ܐܡܗ

i.e. The series of kings is written according to the name of men, instead of women. Joseph the son of David betroths the daughter of David, because the child cannot be enrolled in the name of its mother.

Mösinger, p. 22.

Matt. i. 19. *Joseph, qui vir justus erat, noluit traducere Mariam.* Sed ecce justitia ejus inimica et contraria est legi, quae dixit: Manus tua primum incipiet lapidare eam.

Bar-Ṣalibi *in loc.*

ܘܗܐ ܟܐܢܘܬܗ ܕܗܢܐ
ܣܩܘܒܠܐ ܗܘܬ ܠܢܡܘܣܐ
ܕܐܡܪ ܕܐܝܕܟ ܬܗܘܐ
ܒܗ̇ ܠܘܩܕܡ.

Loftus, p. 36. And behold justice was contrary to the law which saith, Thy hand shall be first upon her.

Mösinger (p. 22).

Multa testimonia habebat [Josephus], Zachariam mutum, Elisabeth praegnantem, angeli annunciationem, exultationem Joannis et prophetiam patrum ejus; haec enim omnia cum aliis multis de conceptione virginis conclamabant.

Isho'dad (f. 182 v.), recounting the things that Mary had laid up in her heart:

ܕܘܨܐ ܕܥܘܠܐ ܕܒܟܪܣܐ.
ܓܠܝܢܐ ܕܠܝܘܣܦ. ܢܒܝܘܬܐ
ܕܙܟܝ ܘܕܒܪܐ. ܘܐܠܝܫܒܥ.
ܣܒܪܬܐ ܕܡܠܐܟܐ ܕܠܘܬܗ̇.

i.e. The exultation of the babe in the womb, the revelation made to Joseph, the prophecy to Zacharias and Elizabeth, and the annunciation of the angel to herself.

And cf. Bar-Ṣalibi *in loc.*

ܬܘܒ ܕܡܛܝܒ ܗܘܐ ܠܗ
ܥܠ ܒܛܢܗ̇ ܕܐܠܝܫܒܥ.

ܘܫܬܩܗ ܕܙܟܪܝܐ. ܘܕܘܨܐ
ܕܝܘܚܢܢ. ܘܐܬܚܫܒ ܕܐܦ
ܗܕܐ ܬܕܡܘܪܬܐ ܗܝ.

Loftus, p. 36. Moreover for that he had heard of Elizabeth's being with child, of Zacharias' loss of speech, and of John's exultation, and he thought also that this was a miracle.

Mösinger, p. 23.

At quomodo fieri potuit, ut ea quae domus fuit et habitatio Spiritus, et cui divina virtus obumbravit, postea conjux mortalis hominis fieret et in doloribus juxta similitudinem primae maledictionis pareret. Quum enim Maria benedicta est in mulieribus, per eam soluta sunt maledicta originalia quibus filii in doloribus et maledictis pariuntur.

cf. Isho'dad (f. 174 v.).

ܠܝܬ ܓܝܪ ܚ̈ܒܠܐ ܓܒ
ܒܬܘܠܬܐ ܕܓܒܪܐ ܠܐ
ܚܟܡܗ ܠܗ̇. ܫܡܐ ܓܝܪ
ܕܒܬܘܠܬܐ ܘܫܡܐ ܕܚ̈ܒܠܐ
ܐܟܚܕܐ ܕܢܗܘܘܢ ܫܪܝܪܝܢ
ܠܐ ܡܟܝܢ.

i.e. For there are no pangs in the case of a virgin that man has not known: the name of virginity and the name of birth pangs cannot be true together.

Bar-Ṣalibi *in loc.*

Loftus, p. 45. And that Joseph did not approach unto her, is evident from the honour due unto her Son, and that she was a Habitacle to the Spirit, and that she received the Vertue of the most High, and that she was the most blessed of women, and that it was indecent she should bring forth with pains and curses.

Mösinger, p. 24.

Sed sicut Dominus intravit portis clausis eodem modo ex utero virginali exiit, quia haec virgo sine partus doloribus realiter et vere peperit.

Imitated by Bar-Ṣalibi.

Loftus, p. 46. If thou requirest proof or illustration, hear how he came forth of the Sepulchre unopened, and entered into the Parlour being shut up; so he came forth of the womb not prejudicing virginity.

Mösinger, p. 24.

Si autem propterea quod quidam discipuli fratres Domini nominantur,

Imitated by Bar-Ṣalibi.

Loftus, p. 46. Although Joses and James and others were called his

existimant hos filios fuisse Mariae, sciant quod et ipse Christus appellatus est filius Josephi, non solum a Judaeis sed et a Maria matre ejus.

Brethren, yet they were not so called as being born of the Virgin, but because they were the sons of Joseph by another wife, and they were in the way of his dispensation called his brethren as Joseph was called his father.

Mösinger, p. 25.

Matt. i. 25, Luke ii. 7. Ipse autem primogenitus nos in baptismo genuit et donis suis primogenitos fecit:

Isho'dad (f. 181 v.).

ܒܘܟܪܐ. ܚܕܐ ܐܝܟ
ܦܬܚ. ܡܪܒܥܐ ܕܐܡܗ:
ܕܬܪܬܝܢ. ܐܝܟ ܕܡܢ
ܡܥܡܘܕܝܬܐ: ܕܬܠܬ ܐܝܟ
ܕܡܢ ܩܝܡܬܐ: ܕܐܪܒܥ.
ܐܝܟ ܪܫܐ ܕܐܚ̈ܐ ܣܓܝ̈ܐܐ.

i.e. The firstborn; (i) as opening the womb of his mother; (ii) from baptism; (iii) from the resurrection; (iv) as the head of many brethren.

Cf. Bar-Ṣalibi *in loc.*

Loftus, p. 46. The firstborn of many brethren, because he hath many brethren from baptism, i.e. to say regeneration.

Mösinger, p. 25.

Matt. i. 25. *Donec peperit primogenitum....* Donec hoc loco non terminum quendam significat, quemadmodum etiam in illo loco: Dixit Dominus domino meo, Sede a dextris meis, donec ponam inimicos sub pedes tuos. Secus enim diceretur, quando inimici sub pedes ejus positi sint, eum surrecturum esse.

Isho'dad (f. 30 r.)

has a mass of similar quotations to prove the same point. Cf. also Bar-Ṣalibi *in loc.*

ܘܡܛܠ ܕܡܠܟ ܡܫܝܚܐ
ܥܕܡܐ ܕܢܣܝܡ ܒܥܠܕܒܒܘܗܝ
ܬܚܝܬ ܪ̈ܓܠܘܗܝ... ܡܕܡ ܗܘ
ܕܥܕܡܐ ܒܗܠܝܢ ܘܠܝܢ
ܘܕܐܝܟ ܗܠܝܢ ܠܐ
ܡܬܚܡܐܝܬ ܐܡܝܪ̈.

Loftus, p. 26. Christ shall reign until he shall put all enemies under his feet: .... wherefore the word 'until' in these and other the like places is not spoken definitely.

Mösinger, p. 26.

Dixit itaque nativitatem Christi in diebus Augusti fuisse. Cur autem prima haec descriptio tempore quo natus est Dominus facta est? Quia scriptum est: Non deficiet princeps Judae neque dominator ex lumbis ejus, donec veniet is cujus peculium est.

Isho'dad (f. 179 r.).

i.e. For he makes mention of Augustus Caesar in order to shew that the prophecy of Jacob was fulfilled that 'the Sceptre shall not pass away, etc.'

Mösinger, p. 27.

Illo igitur tempore venit, quia defecerat rex et propheta.

Isho'dad (f. 179 r.).

i.e. In that Herod completely brought to confusion the kingdom and priesthood of Israel.

Mösinger, p. 27.

In connexion with the account of the visit of the shepherds to Bethlehem, there is room for a suspicion that the commentary contained originally some statement as to the gifts brought by the shepherds. For we find that Isho'dad refers expressly to Mar Ephrem as the source of a statement which he makes with regard to the gifts of the shepherds. The passage is as follows:

Isho'dad (f. 182 v.).

i.e. Mar Ephrem says that the shepherds came with three kinds of gifts: flesh and milk and glory; flesh for Joseph, milk for His mother, and glory for the child; and he says, moreover, that the coming of the Magi was ordered for the self-same day by the wonder-working Divine intimation.

There is something very like this in Ephrem's fifth Sermon *in natalem Domini* (ed. Rom. ii. 418) as follows:

ܠܒܢܘ ܬܘܒ ܘܐܬܐ ܕܪ̈ܘܫܬܐ ܠܦܘܠܓܐ ܕܬܪ̈ܝܢܐ ܫܠܝܐ
ܫܠܝܐ ܒܡܪܝܐ ܕܒܢܐ ܫܡܘܥܝܐ ܦܐܐ. ܦܪܫܘ ܘܡܗܒܘ
ܗܘܘ ܠܗܘܢ ܒܡܪܝܐ. ܠܡܪܝܡ ܫܠܝܐ. ܘܠܡܪܐ ܫܡܘܥܝܐ

The question is, whether this is a mere piece of poetic fancy on Ephrem's part; if so, this must be the passage referred to by Isho'dad; if, on the other hand, Ephrem is working upon some expansion of the gospel narrative, we should expect him also to shew signs of the same in the Commentary on the Diatessaron.

Mösinger, p. 28.

Luke ii. 34. *Et in signum contradictionis et tuam ipsius animum...... pertransibit gladius:* i.e. negatio. [Sed Graecus clare dicit: Revelentur in multis cordibus cogitationes.] *Nimirum eorum qui dubitabant.* Et quod dicit: *Pertransibit gladius*, i.e. et tu dubitabis, quia scilicet credidit eum esse hortulanum. Admirabatur enim, aiunt, Maria et de nativitate et de conceptione ejus atque aliis narravit, quomodo concepit et quare peperit, et nonnulli, admirantes verbum ejus, confortabantur, alii vero erant qui de eo dubitarent.

[Cf. Zahn, *Tatian* p. 61.]

Isho'dad (f. 183 v.).

ܡܪܝ ܐܦܪܝܡ. ܒܢܦܫܟܝ ܠܟܝ
ܬܥܒܪܝܢܗ̇ ܪܘܡܚܐ.
ܕܢܬܠܓܘܢ ܡܢ ܠܒ̈ܘܬܐ
ܕܪ̈ܒܝܐ[1] ܗܘ̈ܢܝܐ ܗܢܘܢ
ܕܐܬܦܠܓܘ. ܗ̄. ܐܦ ܐܢܬܝ
ܬܬܦܠܓܝܢ ܒܗ. ܡܛܠ
ܕܡܬܕܡܪܐ ܒܬܕܡܪ̈ܬܗ
ܘܡܫܬܥܝܐ ܠܐܚܪ̈ܢܐ
ܘܡܫܬܪ̈ܝܢ ܡܢ ܦܘܠܓܐ
ܕܥܠܘܗܝ (Cod. ܕܥܠܘ).

Mar Ephrem: Through thy own soul the spear shall pass, in order that many minds may doubt from the hearts, those namely who doubted: i.e. thou also shalt doubt, because she marvelled at the marvels and related them to others, and they were set free from doubts concerning him.

The reference to the Graecus is by a later hand, for it has displaced the true text in which there must have stood the key-word *dubitare.* And as a matter of fact the desired word is easily restored in the quotation of Isho'dad by the substitution of ܬܬܦܠܓܘܢ for ܬܬܠܓܘܢ.

[1] Read ܪ̈ܒܝܢܐ?

Mary the Virgin is identified with Mary Magdalene, both here and elsewhere in the commentary; the same confusion is found in the Talmud, which calls the mother of our Lord by the name of Miriam the woman's hairdresser, which latter term is an attempt to translate the word Magdalene. (See also Bar-Ṣalibi, who tells us that Mary Magdalene was so called because her hair was plaited.)

The passage in Luke, with the restored word supplied as above, is the key to the understanding of the passage, Mösinger 269, where indeed the verse itself is quoted.

Maria *dubitavit* quando audierat eum surrexisse, et venit et vidit eum et dixit: Si tu sustulisti eum, ideo hoc dixit, ut ei ostenderet, se vere resurrexisse.......sed quia illi *dubitaverunt*, dixit ad eam: Donec ascendo ad Patrem meum, non accedes ad me, ut illud: Tuam ipsius animam pertransibit gladius i.e. denegatio.

Mösinger, p. 31. Ephrem tells us that the Mystery of the Virgin Birth was revealed to Moses, Gideon and Ezekiel. The explanation of this lies in the Burning Bush, the Dew on the Fleece, and the Closed Door of the Sanctuary. Statements to that effect will be found in Ephrem (ed. Rom. iii. 695 for Moses; i. 317 for Gideon; and ed. Lamy, ii. 532 for Ezekiel).

I have no space to discuss at length the parallels between the Commentary and the works of Ephrem: but this passage seemed to require a word of explanation.

Mösinger, p. 31.

Matt. ii. 8. Quemadmodum enim propter Ezechiam signum datum est, quod omnibus vera praedicaret, ut per solem retrogradientem intelligerent, quis ille esset, qui eum a morte ad vitam reduxerat, ita etiam hoc sidus etc.

Isho'dad (f. 34 r.).

ܘܐܝܟܢܐ ܕܠܘ ܒܠܚܘܕ
ܡܛܠ ܚܙܩܝܐ ܐܬܝܗܒܬ
ܐܬܐ. ܐܠܐ ܕܬܬܟܪܙ
ܠܟܠܗ ܒܪܝܬܐ ܒܝܕ ܫܡܫܐ
ܕܗܦܟ ܘܢܕܥܘܢ ܠܒܪܘܝܐ
ܕܟܠ. ܘܠܡܗܦܟܢܗ ܕܚܙܩܝܐ
ܡܢ ܡܘܬܐ ܠܚܝܐ
ܘܡܝܬܪܘܬܗ ܘܫܪܟܐ:

i.e. And just as it was not for the sake of Hezekiah alone that the sign was given but that it might be proclaimed by the sun that returned to the whole creation, and they might know the Creator of all and the one that brought back Hezekiah from death to life, and his excellence, etc.

Mösinger, p. 31.

Matt. ii. 11. *Et aperuerunt thesauros suos et obtulerunt ei munera, aurum* humanitati ejus *et myrrham* morti ejus *et thus* divinitati ejus; vel, *aurum* qua regi *et thus* qua Deo *et myrrham* qua mortali. Rursus *aurum* quia adoratio quae coram auro fiebat reditura erat ad dominum suum, *et myrrham et thus*, quae medicum annunciaverunt, qui vulnus Adami sanaret.

Isho'dad (f. 36 r.).

ܒܝܕ ܕܗܒܐ ܓܝܪ ܕܩܪܒܘ
ܠܗ ܫܘܕܥ. ܚܘܐ ܗܝܢ ܥܠ
ܡܠܟܘܬܗ. ܕܗܒܐ ܗܘ ܓܝܪ
ܩܘܪܒܢܐ ܕܡܠܟ̈ܐ........
.... ܒܝܕ ܡܘܪܐ ܕܝܢ ܐܪܙܘ
ܥܠ ܚܫܐ ܕܐܢܫܘܬܗ....
ܬܘܒ. ܒܝܕ ܡܘܪܐ ܒܕܩܘ
ܕܐܣܝܐ ܗܘ ܕܡܐܣܐ
ܫܚ̈ܩܬܗ ܕܐܕܡ.....
ܒܠܒܘܢܬܐ ܕܝܢ ܫܘܕܥ[1]
ܚܘܐ ܥܠ ܐܠܗܘܬܗ.

i.e. By the gold which they offered to him, he intimated, (i) concerning his kingdom, for gold is the offering to kings......: by the myrrh they signified the sufferings of his humanity; ......again by the myrrh they ascertained that he is the physician who heals the wounds of Adam...by the frankincense they intimated, first, of his divinity.

Cf. Bar-Ṣalibi *in loc.*

Loftus, p. 63. According to their custom they offered these gifts, for they were accustomed to burn incense to their gods and to give gold to their kings and to embalm their dead with myrrh; and forasmuch as they understood that he was God and a king and that he was to die and to be anointed they offered him these gifts: Frankincense in relation to his divinity; gold, in relation to the majesty of a king, and myrrh to his death, the cause of life. Moreover, gold denotes that worship, which is preferred be-

[1] Read ܫܘܕܥܘ.

fore gold, is returned to its Lord: myrrh and incense signify that he is the physician and binds up the wounds and fractures of Adam.

Cf. Bar-Hebraeus *in loc.*

ܕܗܒܐ ܐܝܟ ܕܠܡܠܟܐ.
ܘܡܘܪܐ ܐܝܟ ܕܠܗܘ ܕܥܬܝܕ
ܠܡܡܬ ܥܠ ܐܦ̈ܘܗܝ
ܕܥܠܡܐ. ܘܠܒܘܢܬܐ ܐܝܟ
ܕܠܐܠܗܐ.

Gold as to a king, and myrrh as to Him who is about to die for the world, and frankincense as to God.

Bar-Salibi (or is it Loftus ?) has not understood the meaning of the worship which was made to gold (probably, as Mösinger suggests, to the golden calf), and has explained it to mean that worship is preferred before gold (ܣܓܕܬܐ ܩܕܡ ܕܗܒܐ). Otherwise he follows Ephrem closely. The mystical interpretations of the gold, myrrh and frankincense (in this order in Western texts) go back to a very early time, and are given by many of the early fathers. Especially note Irenaeus (ed. Mass. 184).

"Myrrham quidem, quod ipse erat, qui pro mortali humano genere moreretur et sepeliretur: Aurum vero, quoniam Rex, cujus Regni finis non est: Thus vero, quoniam Deus, etc."

In connexion with the account of the coming of the Magi, note that, according to the Syrian commentators, it was the opinion of Mar Ephrem that the Magi came to Bethlehem two years after the birth of Christ. And the question arises as to whether they deduced this opinion from the Commentary on the Gospel or from other parts of Mar Ephrem's writings. That such was the opinion of Ephrem is certain from such statements as the following from his Hymn on the Nativity (ed. Lamy, ii. p. 495):

ܫܢܐ ܫܢܬ ܬܪ̈ܬܝܢ ܕܠܒܗ ܕܦܪ̈ܣܝܢ
ܡܠܘܫ̈ܐ ܦܣܝ̈ܩܝܢ ܒܗ
ܦܪ̈ܫܐ ܡܡܢ̈ܝܢ ܒܗ

etc.

i.e. In the second year from the birth of our Saviour
The Magi rejoiced,
The Pharisees were sad.

But the arrangement of the text in the Commentary shews that not only did Ephrem hold this view that the visit of the Magi was later than that of the shepherds, but that Tatian held something like the same opinion; for the text interposes the presentation of Christ in the temple between the story of the shepherds and the arrival of the Magi; and in the Arabic Harmony the latter incident not only begins a fresh chapter but is introduced by a significant *post haec*. So that we may say that Ephrem was invited to hold the opinion by the arrangement of the text upon which he was commenting, in which the Magi are posterior to the shepherds, and where the interval of two years would be suggested by the statement in Matt. ii. 16 that Herod slew all the children from two years and under according to the time that he had accurately enquired from the Magi.

Let us now see what the later commentators say on the point: first of all we have the testimony of Bar-Ṣalibi.

Bar-Ṣalibi tells us as follows (sec. Loftum):

i.e. "He said, From two years old and under, because he enquiring of the Wise-men, they answered him, It was two years since the star appeared unto us; therefore said the Lord Ephraim and Eusebius, that the Wise-men came in the second year of our Lord's nativity. And the Lord John [i.e. Chrysostom] and St Cyril say that the star appeared two years before, and that the Wise-men tarried long before they came in the way[1]."

Bar-Hebraeus is not very different, though he adds somewhat to the list of authorities:

[Syriac text, four lines]

i.e. And St John [Chrysostom] and Cyril say that they came when he was a babe and wrapped in swaddling-clothes, from the fact that the star led them before he was born; and Eusebius and Epiphanius and Mar Ephrem

[1] Loftus, p. 71.

and Mar Jacob say that after two years, when they brought him up to Jerusalem and when they were at Bethlehem, the Magi came.

The question then is whether Ephrem says definitely in his Commentary what is attributed to him by the later writers and what is certainly found elsewhere in his works. And in answer to this question we may say that not only is it involved in Ephrem's interpretation that the visit of the Magi was at a later period than that of the shepherds, but we also find that at a subsequent place in the Commentary he reverts to the destruction of the children by Herod and says that Christ was two years old at the time. The reference will be found at p. 40 of Mösinger in the words: 'Sed cum duorum esset annorum hoc ei facere (sc. occidere) cogitarant cum suo principe Herode.'

Mösinger, p. 32.	Bar-Ṣalibi *in loc.*
Matt. ii. 16. Herodes nescivit, qua ratione eam exploraret, obcaecatus enim aemulatione ad cognitionem pervenire nequivit: .... Licet haec omnia novisset, tamen aemulatione inebriatus cum cognoscendo impar fuit.	ܐܠܐ ܟܝܢܗ ܗܘ ܚܣܡܐ ܕܢܣܡܐ ܠܬܪܥܝܬܐ ܕܠܐ ܬܚܙܐ ܥܠܬܐ. i.e. (sec. Loftum, p. 62) "It is the nature of Envy to blind the understanding so as not to discern reason."

Mösinger, p. 34.	Bar-Ṣalibi *in loc.*
Matt. ii. 18. Scriptum est enim: Mortua est Rachel stadio uno ad introitum in Ephrata quod est Bethlehem. .... Quumque Samuel Sauli signum daret, quando unxit eum regem super Israel, dixit ei: Ecce, occurrent tibi tres viri in Zelzach apud sepulchrum Rachelis in confinibus Benjamin.	ܐܡܪ ܫܡܘܐܝܠ ܠܫܐܘܠ. ܕܗܐ ܦܓܥܝܢ ܒܟ ܬܠܬܐ ܓܒܪܝܢ ܒܨܠܨܚ ܥܠ ܓܒ ܩܒܪܗ ܕܪܚܝܠ ܒܬܚܘܡܗ ܕܒܢܝܡܝܢ. ܬܘܒ ܘܪܚܝܠ ܡܩܒܪܐ ܡܪܕܐ ܦܪܣܝܐ ܡܢ ܐܦܪܬ ܕܗܝ ܒܒܝܬ ܠܚܡ. which Loftus renders as follows: Samuel said unto Saul, Three men are to meet thee in Tsaltsach near Rachel's sepulchre in the border of Benjamin; Rachel was buried a Persian day's journey from Ephrata which is in Bethlehem. [Corr. 'a Persian day's journey' to 'a parasang.']

Mösinger, p. 35.

Persecutionem passus est David a
Saul, sicut et Filius ejus ab Herode.
Interfecti sunt sacerdotes propter
David, et infantes propter Dominum
nostrum; ex sacerdotibus Abiathar
liber evasit, sicut Joannes ex infanti-
bus.   In Abiathar ablatum est sacerdotium domus Heli et in Joanne
ablata est prophetia filiorum Jacob.

Isho'dad (f. 21 r.).

(Syriac text)

i.e. David was persecuted by Saul,
as also was the Son by Herod. The
priests were slain on account of David,
and the children on account of our
Lord. Of the priests Abiathar es-
caped, and of the children John....In
Abiathar the priesthood of the house
of Eli came to nought; and in John
the prophecy of the sons of Jacob
ceased.

Mösinger, p. 36.

Matt. ii. 23. Et quod dicit: *Nazoraenus vocabitur*, quia nimirum virga
Hebraice Nazor sonat et propheta
eum vocat filium Nazor (filium virgae)
quoniam revera virgae filius est. Sed
Evangelista, quod in Nazareth nutri-
tus est, huic simile esse videns dixit,
Nazoraenus vocabitur.

Isho'dad (f. 38 r.).

(Syriac text)

¹ Cod. adds *(Syriac word)* ex errore.

i.e. It was known and he set it down from the grace of the Spirit. Again, a rod in Hebrew is called Nazor, and the city was called Nazareth, a rod; the passage of Isaiah, There shall sprout a rod from his root, is written in Hebrew Nazor.

Bar-Ṣalibi *in loc.*

i.e. 'When Matthew saw that Christ came and dwelt in Nazareth he expounded this of Esaiah, A Branch shall sprout out, He shall be called a Nazaren: and he was called a Nazaren from Nazareth, that is, ܢܘܪܒܐ *one sprouting out*, from ܢܘܪܒܬܐ *a sprout;* so they are expounded in the Hebrew tongue.' (Loftus, p. 79.)

Cf. Bar-Hebraeus *in loc.*

ܘܡܪܝ ܐܦܪܝܡ ܐܡܪ. ܕܠܘܚܐ ܐܘܟܝܬ ܢܘܪܒܐ ܢܨܘܪ ܡܬܩܪܐ ܒܥܒܪܐܝܬ. ܒܪܡ ܗܝ ܗܕܐ ܢܒܝܘܬܐ ܗܝ ܕܢܦܘܩ ܠܘܚܐ ܡܢ ܫܪܫܐ ܕܐܝܫܝ ܐܬܝܠܗ. ܘܡܢ ܗܪܟܐ ܗܝ ܕܢܨܪܝܐ ܡܬܩܪܐ.

i.e. And Mar Ephrem says: That the rod, i.e. the branch is called in Hebrew Nosor; this is therefore the prophecy that 'A rod shall come out of the root of Jesse,' and it is hence that he is called Nazarene.

Ephrem plays on the same string in his Hymns to the Virgin Mary (ed. Lamy, ii. p. 539):

ܗܘܬ ܡܪܝܡ ܓܦܬܐ ܘܦܪܥ ܡܢܗ̇ ܢܘܪܒܐ ܢܨܪܝܐ ܐܝܟ ܕܟܬܝܒ ܕܢܫܠܡ ܐܪܙܐ ܕܢܒܝܘܬܐ ܒܢܨܪܬ ܐܬܪܒܝ ܕܢܫܠܡ ܟܠ.

i.e. Mary was the Vine, and there sprang from her the Nazarene branch, according as it is written; that he might fulfil the mystery of the prophecy, he was brought up in Nazareth, that he might fulfil all things.

The dependence of the later commentators on Ephrem is involved in their statements as well as in the express ascription by Bar-Hebraeus.

To the foregoing may be added the marginal note quoted by Zahn (*Tatian*, p. 46) from Cod. Vat. Syr. 268, as described by Adler in *N. T. Verss. Syrr.* p. 81:

ܡܢ ܟܬܒܐ ܕܠܐ ܝܕܝܥܐ. ܐܝܟ ܕܝܢ ܚܣܝܐ
ܡܪܝ ܐܦܪܝܡ ܗܘ ܕܢܦܘܩ ܢܘܪܒܐ ܡܢ ܚܘܛܪܐ
ܕܐܝܫܝ ܗܘ ܢܘܪܒܐ ܠܡ ܒܥܒܪܐܝܬ ܢܘܨܪܗ ܡܬܩܪܐ.

i.e. [The prophecy that he shall be called a Nazarene] is from an unknown book. But according to the holy Mar Ephrem it is the passage that there shall come a rod out of the stem of Jesse. This rod is in Hebrew called Nosorah.

Mösinger, p. 40.

Matt. iii. 9. Ex lapidibus istis Deus potest suscitare filios Abrahami, i.e. ex adoratoribus lapidum et lignorum. Sicut et dicit: Patrem multarum gentium feci te.

Isho'dad (f. 40 v.).

ܐܘ ܡܢ ܣܓܘ̈ܕܝ ܠܟܐ̈ܦܐ
ܘܩܝ̈ܣܐ. ܐܒܐ ܠܡ
ܠܣܘܓܐܐ ܕܥܡ̈ܡܐ
ܣܡܬܟ.

i.e. Or from the worshippers of stones and stocks. I have set thee for a father to the multitude of the nations.

Mösinger, p. 42.

Dominus noster dextram ejus sumpsit et super caput suum posuit.

Isho'dad (f. 43 r.).

ܐܚܪ̈ܢܐ. ܕܟܕ ܪܬܝܬ ܠܡ
ܣܡ ܐܝܕܗ ܥܠ ܪܝܫܗ ܕܡܪܗ.

i.e. Others say: that he laid his hand tremblingly on the head of his Lord.

It is not easy to determine whether this is Tatian or Ephrem; but I incline to think that it is the former. As will be seen, the story was known to Isho'dad, and it will also be found in Bar-Ṣalibi, though Bar-Ṣalibi does not know from whence it is taken. 'From whence, says he, is it known that John put his hand on the head of Christ, when no such thing is written in the Gospel?' And we say that it is from the Old Testament, from the passage where the Lord said to Moses, 'I will cover thee with my hand,' and from this, that 'Moses put his hands upon Aaron and anointed him and consecrated him.'

The laying on of hands is implied also in the statement made a little lower down that 'per Joannem enim propheticam et sacerdotalem dignitatem accepit.'

The Maronite breviary (ed. 1665) shews an acquaintance with the statement that John laid his hand on the head of Christ, as well as with the previously quoted description of John as the one who betrothed the Church to Christ. In the festival of the Decollation of the Baptist we are told

ܘܡܟܪ ܠܗ ܥܕܬܐ ܩܕܝܫܬܐ ܠܒܪ ܐܠܗܐ ܕܨܒܐ
ܘܐܬܡܟܟ. ܘܣܡ ܝܡܝܢܗ ܥܠ ܪܝܫܗ ܒܡܥܡܕܢܘܬܗ.
ܐܪܟܢ ܪܝܫܗ ܡܪܗ ܕܥܠܡܐ ܬܚܝܬ ܐܝܕܗ.

i.e. And he betrothed to the Son of God the Holy Church, to Him who was willing and humbled Himself: and he put his right hand on His head at His baptism; the Lord of the World bowed His head beneath the hand of John.

(The sentences are probably due to Ephrem.)

Mösinger, p. 43.

Quumque ex lumine super aquas exorto et ex voce de caelo delapso, etc.

Isho'dad (f. 43 r.).

ܘܡܚܕܐ ܐܝܟ ܕܣܗܕ
ܕܝܐܛܣܪܘܢ ܢܘܗܪܐ ܐܕܢܚ.
ܘܥܠ ܝܘܪܕܢ ܐܬܦܪܣ ܥܢ̈ܢܐ
ܚܘܪ̈ܬܐ. ܘܐܬܚܙܝܘ ܣܓܝ̈ܐܬܐ
ܡܫܪ̈ܝܬܐ ܪ̈ܘܚܢܝܐ ܕܡܫܒܚܝܢ
ܒܐܐܪ. ܘܫܠܝ ܒܫܠܝܘܬܐ
ܘܝܘܪܕܢ ܡܢ ܡܪܕܝܬܗ ܟܕ
ܫܠܝܢ ܡܘ̈ܗܝ. ܘܪܝܚܐ
ܕܒܣܝ̈ܡܐ ܡܢ ܬܡܢ ܢܫܒ
ܗܘܐ.

i.e. And straightway, as the Diatessaron testifies, light shone forth, and over the Jordan was spread a vail of white clouds, and there appeared many hosts of spiritual beings who were praising God in the air; and quietly Jordan stood still from its flowing, its waters being at rest; and a sweet odour was wafted from thence.

[Note that the Syriac Lexicographers (Payne Smith col. 1584) connect the name Jordan with the shining of light, so that they betray their knowledge of the legend by equating

ܝܘܪܕܢ = ܢܘܗܪܐ ܕܢܚ ܠܗ

Cf. Mt. iv. 16 φῶς ἀνέτειλεν αὐτοῖς and Nestle's note in *Gött. Gelehrte Anzeigen*, 1894. 2. p. 85.]

From the reference to the light which shone at the Jordan, it was at least a probable hypothesis that the text of Tatian had some traces of the peculiar amplifications of the account of the Baptism which are current in early copies, versions and fathers. This hypothesis is now rendered reasonably certain by the direct testimony of Isho'dad. It is not necessary to suppose that the whole of the extract which we have given from Isho'dad is from Tatian. Probably the quotation is contained in the first clause, or, at most, in the words:

ܡܚܘܝܐ ܢܘܗܪܐ ܐܝܟ ܥܠ ܝܘܪܕܢ

Mösinger, p. 40.

Ad puteum Eliezer Rebeccam, ad puteum Jacob Rachelem, ad puteum Moyses Sephoram desponsavit. Qui omnes typi erant Domini nostri, qui ecclesiam in baptismo Jordanis sponsam sibi fecit. Quemadmodum Eliezer ad fontem stans monstravit Rebeccae dominum ejus Isaac, qui tunc temporis in agrum prodibat, ut ei obviam veniret, ita et Joannes de fonte Jordanis fluvii Salvatorem nostrum monstravit.

Isho'dad (f. 250 v.).

ܡܪܝ ܐܦܪܝܡ. ܟܕ ܡܚܘܐ
ܕܛܘܦܣܐ ܕܡܘܬܐ ܩܢܐ ܠܩܘܫܬܐ
ܣܓܝ ܬܪܝܨܐ ܐܡܪ. ܐܠܝܥܙܪ
ܠܡ ܡܟܘܪܗ̇ ܕܪܦܩܐ ܚܘܝܗ̇
ܠܐܝܣܚܩ ܟܕ ܐܬܐ ܒܚܩܠܐ
ܠܐܘܪܥܗܘܢ ܘܝܘܚܢܢ
ܡܟܘܪܗ̇ ܕܥܕܬܐ ܚܘܝܗ̇
ܠܚܬܢܐ ܡܟܝܪܗ̇. ܕܐܬܐ
ܠܘܬܗ̇ ܥܠ ܝܘܪܕܢ ܢܘܗܪܐ.
ܡܟܝܠ ܐܠܝܥܙܪ ܠܪܦܩܐ ܥܠ
ܒܪܐ ܕܡܪ̈ܝܐ. ܘܥܠ ܒܪܐ
ܕܡܪ̈ܝܐ ܡܟܝܠ ܡܘܕܥ ܠܢܫܐ.
ܘܥܠ ܒܪܐ ܕܡܪ̈ܝܐ ܡܟܝܠ
ܡܘܕܥܐ ܠܝܘܚܢܢ. ܘܥܠ
ܢܘܗܪܐ ܕܡܪ̈ܝܐ ܡܟܝܠ ܡܘܚܝܢ
ܠܥܠܡܐ.

Mar Ephrem, shewing that the type possesses great likeness to the reality, says: Eliezer, indeed, who betrothed Rebecca, shewed to her Isaac when he came to meet them in the field; and John who betrothed the Church, shewed to her the bridegroom her spouse who came to her at the river Jordan. Eliezer betrothed Rebecca at the well of water; at the well of water Jacob betrothed Rachel: and at the well of water Moses betrothed Zippora; and at the river of water John betrothed the Church.

Bar-Ṣalibi abbreviates the passage as follows: i.e. (Loftus, p. 88) By water were made the Espousals of Rebecca, of Rachel and Tsiphora, typifying the Water of Baptism by which the Church is espoused.

It is interesting to notice that Isho'dad, while confessedly transcribing from Ephrem, corrects Ephrem's mistake in making Eliezer *stand by the well* and point out Isaac to Rebecca.

Mösinger, p. 41.

Ecce, hic est agnus Dei, hic est, qui venit, tollere peccata mundi.

The Commentary belonging to this passage has disappeared, except for the words inserted 'hic est qui venit,' which are explained in Isho'dad: probably Isho'dad's comment is directly from Ephrem, having been lost in the Armenian text.

It may, of course, be held that the words 'hic est qui venit' are a part of the text of Tatian, and not of the commentary of Ephrem. On p. 43 we find again, Ecce venit agnus Dei et is est qui tollit peccata mundi.

Isho'dad (f. 250 v.)
following the previous quotation:

ܘܓܠܝܐ ܗܘ ܠܒܪ ܕܗܘ
ܕܐܡܪ ܕܗܐ ܐܡܪܗ ܕܐܠܗܐ.
ܥܠ ܕܡܣܟܝܢ ܗܘܘ ܠܗ. ܘܟܕ
ܕܝܢ ܐܬܐ ܡܚܘܐ ܗܘܐ
ܠܗ ܐܝܟ ܕܒܨܒܥܐ ܠܗܘܢ
ܕܩܪܝܒܝܢ.

i.e. For this is clear that what he said 'Behold the Lamb of God' was because they were expecting him: and when he came, he was pointing him out as with fingers to them that were near.

Mösinger, p. 52.

Factae sunt nuptiae in Cana Galilaeorum. Et cum Dominus eo veniret, dicit ad eum mater: Vinum non habent hic. Dicit ei Jesus: Quid est mihi et tibi, mulier? Non mihi tempus advenit: id est, ego non vi eis me ingero, sed ipsi animadvertant,

Isho'dad (f. 252 v.).

ܡܪܝ ܐܦܪܝܡ ܪܒܐ.
ܕܡܫܬܥܐ ܗܘܐ ܠܗ ܠܡ
ܡܛܠܗ ܕܐܬܐ ܠܘܬܗ ܕܢܒܒ
ܬܡܢ. ܘܥܠ ܗܕܐ ܦܝ ܠܗ

vinum defecisse et omnes bibere expectent; idque dixit, ut donum suum in oculis eorum gloriosum appareret.

ܟܕ ܐܦܝܣܬܗ. ܕܚܣܪ ܠܗ
ܚܡܪܐ. ܡܢܐ ܠܝ[1] ܘܠܟܝ
ܐܢܬܬܐ. ܠܐ ܠܗ ܦܐܝܐ
ܕܐܢܐ ܡܢ ܩܛܝܪ ܐܙܠ
ܠܘܬܗܘܢ ܐܠܐ ܢܪܓܫܘܢ
ܟܠܗܘܢ ܕܚܣܪ ܚܡܪܐ
ܘܢܫܐܠܘܢ[2] ܠܡܫܬܐ. ܐܝܟ
ܕܬܬܪܒ ܡܘܗܒܬܗ ܕܐܠܗܐ
ܒܥܝܢܝܗܘܢ.

Mar Ephrem the great says: that she had heard from him that he was about to work a miracle, and therefore he answered her when she persuaded him that the wine had failed, What have I to do with thee, woman? Certainly it is not proper for me to go to them by force, but let them all feel that the wine has failed, and let them ask to drink in order that the gift of God may be magnified in their sight.

Mösinger, p. 53.

Et quum mater hoc ei dixisset, respondit Jesus: Non mihi tempus advenit: id est, certe advenit.

Isho'dad (f. 253 r.).

ܘܐܠܐ ܠܐ ܟܕܫܠ ܐܬܬ
ܫܥܬܝ. ܗ̄. ܐܝܢ ܠܗ
ܐܬܬ ܫܥܬܝ.

Mösinger, p. 57.

Noe super altare, in monte Corduaeorum exstructum, sacrificium obtulit.

The passage is certainly from a Syriac hand, (cf. Peshito of Gen. viii. 4), and can easily be restored to its primitive form. Mösinger refers to a similar statement in Ephrem's Commentary on Genesis (Vol. I. p. 152). We may add Ephr. (ed. Lamy, i. 711) *Hymni de Crucifixione:*

[1] Cod. ܠܢ.   [2] Cod. ܘܢܫܐܠܘܢ.

ܡܢ ܛܘܪ̈ܝ ܩܪܕܘ
ܠܩܛܬ ܠܒܣܡ̈ܝܗ
ܕܡܢ ܬܡܢ ܢܘܚ ܘܫܝܡ ....

i.e. From the mountains of Kardu
She has gathered flowers;
From thence come Noah and Shem, etc.

Mösinger, p. 59.

Tota nocte laboravimus, quibus verbis doctrina Prophetarum significatur, de excelso missa in mundum qui per mare repraesentatus est. Duae naves sunt circumcisio et praeputium. Et quod innuerunt sociis suis, mysterium est septuaginta duorum discipulorum, quia Apostoli piscaturae et messi non sufficiebant.

Isho'dad (f. 189 v.).

ܡܪܝ ܐܦܪܝܡ: ܠܠܝܐ ܠܡ
ܐܪܙ ܦܘܠܚܢܐ (l. ܝܘܠܦܢܐ)
ܕܢܒܝ̈ܐ ܘܕܫܠܝ̈ܚܐ ܕܒܥܡܐ.
ܕܐܚܫܟ ܣܘܟܠܗ. ܘܝܘܠܦܢܗ
ܕܝܢ ܢܦܠ ܡܢ ܪܘܡܐ ܠܥܠܡܐ[1]
ܕܡܬܠ ܒܝܡܐ.
ܗ. ܣܦܝܢ̈ܐ ܬܪ̈ܬܝܢ
ܓܙܘܪܬܐ ܘܥܘܪܠܘܬܐ.
ܓܒܐ ܕܝܡܝܢܐ ܡܢ ܣܦܝܢܬܐ
ܠܣܦܝܢܬܐ. ܘܪܡܙܘ
ܠܚܒܪ̈ܝܗܘܢ ܐܪܙ ܫܒܥܝܢ
ܘܬܪ̈ܝܢ. ܕܒܨܝܪܝܢ ܗܘܘ ܓܝܪ
ܗܘܘ ܠܨܝܕܐ ܘܠܚܨܕܐ.

The night signifies the teaching of the prophets and the apostles, which is among the people the understanding of which is darkened; but the teaching falls from on high into the world which is compared with the sea. The two ships are the circumcision and the uncircumcision. The right hand side from ship to ship (?). And that they beckoned to their companions signifies the 72 disciples; for they were inadequate for the fishing and the harvest.

[1] Cod. ܠܥܠܡܡܐ (sic !).

Note that the comparison between the sea and the world is a favourite one with Ephrem. The passage is given almost exactly in Isho'dad, and there is an added sentence to interpret the 'right side of the ship' which seems to have dropped out of the Armenian text, and is in its present form scarcely intelligible in the Syriac.

Mösinger, p. 61.

Matt. ix. 15. Omne illud tempus, quod Dominus noster in hac terra transegit, thalamo comparat et se ipsum sponso.

Bar-Ṣalibi *in loc.*

ܚܬܢܐ ܠܢܦܫܗ ܩܪܐ.
ܓܢܘܢܐ ܠܡܬܚܬܢܘܬܗ ܕܥܠ
ܐܪܥܐ.

i.e. (sec. Loftum) Seipsum appellat sponsum, descensum aut durationem suam super terram thalamum.

Mösinger, p. 63.

Matt. v. 6. Beatus, qui esurit et sitit justitiam, sicuti dicit: Non esurit panem, nec sitit aquam, sed esurit et sitit ut audiat verbum Domini.

The passage quoted is Amos viii. 11, of which the Peshito text is

ܠܐ ܕܟܦܢ ܠܠܚܡܐ ܘܠܐ
ܕܨܗܝܐ ܠܡܝ̈ܐ ܐܠܐ ܠܡܫܡܥ
ܡܠܬܗ ܕܡܪܝܐ.

Mösinger wrongly supposes a reference to Is. xlix. 10.

The same reference to Amos is implied on p. 44: Esuriit...simulque verbis suis nos docuit in ejusmodi circumstantiis solum verbum Domini nos esurire debere.

Implied in
Isho'dad (f. 208 r.)
[on the prodigal son in want].

ܒܚܣܝܪܘܬܐ ܕܝܢ ܠܒܘܪ̈ܟܬܐ
ܘܒܛܠܢܘܬܐ ܕܝܢ ܕܝܕܥܬܐ
ܕܐܠܗܐ. ܐܫܕܪ ܠܗ ܟܦܢܐ
ܒܐܪܥܐ. ܠܐ ܕܠܠܚܡܐ
ܘܠܐ ܕܡܝ̈ܐ ܐܠܐ ܠܡܫܡܥ.
ܘܓܘ:

By a defect of blessings, and a deprivation of the knowledge of God: 'I will send a hunger on the earth, not of bread nor of water, but of hearing, etc.'

Bar-Ṣalibi *in loc.*

ܐܘ ܟܡ ܗܝ ܕܟܦܢ ܠܕܒܚܬܐ
ܕܐܠܗܐ ܘܫܘܠܦܢܐ ܐܝܟ
ܗܝ ܕܠܐ ܕܟܦܢ ܠܠܚܡܐ ܘܠܐ

ܗܘ̇ܝ ܠܚܡܐ ܐܠܐ
ܠܫܡܥܗ ܒܡܠܬ ܐܠܗܐ.

(sec. Loftum.) Or for that [hunger]
whereby one coveteth the knowledge
of God and His doctrine, according to
that 'He was hungry not for bread
but for the hearing of the word of
God.'

Bar-Hebraeus *in loc.*

ܠܐܝܠܝܢ ܕܟܦܢܝܢ ܘܨܗܝܢ.
ܗ̇. ܠܝܘܠܦܢܐ ܕܚܝܐ ܐܝܟ
ܡܐ. ܕܟܬܝܒ ܕܠܐ ܗܘܐ
ܠܠܚܡܐ ܐܠܐ ܠܫܡܥܗ
ܒܡܠܬ ܐܠܗܐ.

i.e. Those who hunger and thirst :
viz. after the doctrine of life, as it is
written, Who hunger, not for bread,
but for the hearing of the word of
God.

Mösinger, p. 72.	Bar-Hebraeus *in loc.*
Nolite judicare : h.e. injusto ; ne judicemini, h.e. ob injustitiam.	ܠܐ ܬܕܘܢܘܢ. ܗ. ܥܘܠܐܝܬ. ܕܠܐ ܬܬܕܝܢܘܢ. ܗ. ܟܐܢܐܝܬ.

Ye shall not judge ; i.e. wickedly ;
that ye may not be judged ; i.e. righteously.

Mösinger, p. 72.   Isho'dad (f. 56 r.).

Matt. vi. 23. *Si lumen, quod in te
est, tenebrae sunt;* i.e. si per eleemos-
ynas, quae lucidae sunt, peccas,
quanto magis per peccata quae ob-
tenebrant. Adulterium et blasphemia
ex una tantum parte spectari possunt,
quia nihil aliud sunt, quam causae
transgressionum, eleemosynae autem
duplicem habent faciem, quippe quae,
si humanae gloriae causa dantur, ad
transgressionem perducunt, si autem
manus datoris ad fratrem indigentem
ex charitate se extendunt, etiam cogitationes ad Deum, qui retribuit,
pertingent ut Scriptura dicit: Ubi
thesauri vestri sunt, ibi erunt et
corda vestra.

The passage is a difficult one, and
Mösinger has corrected one of his
MSS. from the other, without in-
timating what the text was which he
found to be unintelligible. The Syriac
is fairly clear; two words seem to be
repeated by accident, which we have
bracketed, and it is possible that
some connecting words may have
dropped.

i.e. Mar Ephrem. If thy light
which is in thee, etc. If namely
thou sinnest by thy alms which is
illuminating, i.e. justifying, how
much more by the sin which is
darkening. For adultery and blasphemy have only one side, that
they are sinful; but alms has two
sides. If it is given in human vain-
glory, it makes the man to sin: but
if the hand of the giver is stretched
out to the needy, his thought is
extended towards God the recom-
penser; this is what is meant by
'Where thy treasure is there also, etc.'

Mösinger, p. 74.

Matt. viii. 20....Quia ille vidit mortuos surgentes et mutos loquentes, secum cogitavit, ei cui talia opera sunt, multum etiam esse argenti, ideoque dixit: *Veniam et sequar te.* Propterea responsum accepit: Vulpibus sunt habitacula, ei autem nec id est, quod habent vulpes, scilicet habitaculum.

Imitated by Isho'dad (f. 58 v.).

i.e. He was sick with the love of money, like Judas: for he supposed that the person who receives from our Lord power to work miracles, will also gather from thence plenty of money....In destitution I surpass the beasts and the birds; for they have certain places in which they can hide; but I have not even a certain dwelling place.

Mösinger, p. 91

Nolite ait *possidere aurum* ne in vobis Judas inveniatur et id quod Achar vita privavit et Giezi lepra obtexit.

Abbrev. by Bar-Salibi.

i.e. (Loftus) alio modo sic: *nec possidebitis aurum*, ne similes essent Acano, Gehezi et Judae.

Mösinger, p. 91.

Matt. x. 10. Et quod dixit: *Virgam,*
in signum nimirum regiminis et
humilitatis. *Non baculum* quia non
ad gregem furientem pascendum exi-
erunt, sicut quondam Moyses.

Bar-Salibi *in loc.*

[Syriac text]

i.e. And no scrip, a sign of simplicity
and mark of humility; and no club,
for they were not going forth like
Moses, to feed flocks.

Mösinger, p. 97.

Matt. x. 29. Duo passeres asse
veneunt; duo, non unus. Ostendere
voluit vilitatem passeris. Quae enim
majoris pretii sunt, singula veneunt,
quae vero vilia, multa simul quasi
olera venundantur.

Isho'dad (f. 198 v.).

[Syriac text]

i.e. Matthew said that two sparrows
are sold for a farthing, where Luke
has, five sparrows are sold for two
farthings. He shews the cheapness
of sparrows, for those things that
are superior in value are sold one by
one, but those of less value similarly
are sold like vegetables.

Mösinger, p. 97.

Matt. x. 34. *Nolite putare, quod veni mittere pacem in terra.* Ubi ergo est
illud, quod omnibus dicitur, Christus
venit, ut pacificaret id quod in caelo,
et id quod in terra est. Certo Dominus pacem praedicavit, ut et Apos-
tolus dicit; Fecit nobis pacem: et

Imitated by Bar-Hebraeus *in loc.*

[Syriac text]

alio loco, Qui eum receperunt, pax super eos. Verum alia ex parte non misit pacem, propterea quod fideles ab infidelibus per eum separati sunt. *Veni separare hominem a patre, etc.* Separantur, ait, mente, quia in fide nunquam recte cogitant, quum unus sic Deum colit, alius vero aliter.

ܕܗܘܘ ܥܡܝ. ܘܠܗܝ. ܕܫܠܡܐ
ܕܠܐ ܝܗܒ ܐܢܐ ܠܟܘܢ...

i.e. Some say, How does this agree with the passage, He shall speak peace with the Gentiles; or with this, He is the Lord of peace; or this, He is our peace; or this, My peace I give unto you?

Isho'dad, f. 66 r.

ܗܝ ܕܠܐ ܐܬܝܬ ܕܐܪܡܐ
ܫܝܢܐ ܐܠܐ ܚܪܒܐ. ܘܐܝܟܢܐ
ܗܝ ܗܝ ܕܟܠܗ ܕܐܬܐ
(l. ܐܬܐ) ܕܢܫܝܡ ܥܡ ܐܒܐ
ܕܒܫܡܝܐ. ܘܥܡ ܕܒܐܪܥܐ.

. . . .

ܘܗܘܝܘ ܠܡ ܫܝܢܢ...
ܘܠܐܝܠܝܢ ܕܡܩܒܠܝܢ ܠܗ ܫܝܢܐ
ܗܘܐ. ܐܠܐ ܥܠ ܕܐܬܦܠܓܘ
ܡܗܝܡܢܐ ܡܢ ܠܐ
ܡܗܝܡܢܐ... ܕܐܒܗܬܐ
ܢܬܦܠܓܘܢ ܥܠ ܒܢܝܗܘܢ.
ܥܠ ܕܠܐ ܗܝܡܢܘ ܒܡܫܝܚܐ.
ܘܒܢܝܐ ܢܬܚܪܘܢ ܥܡ
ܐܒܗܝܗܘܢ. ܥܠ ܕܫܒܩܘ
ܕܚܠܬܐ ܕܐܒܗܝܗܘܢ.

i.e. This passage 'I am not come to send peace on the earth but a sword,' how does it agree with the words, He came to reconcile all that is in heaven and that is in earth... and 'he is our peace'...and 'to those that receive him, there is peace.' But that believers were separated from unbelievers...that the fathers should be divided against the children, because they did not believe in Christ; and children shall contend with their parents, because they have left the worship of their fathers.

Mösinger, p. 99.

Matt. xi. 3. *Tu es qui venturus es, an alium exspectamus.* Nequaquam dubitavit de eo. Qui enim in deserto viam paravit, nec cunctatus est in ventre exultare, qui in baptismo nullam sibi gloriam attribuit, quia dicebat; Me oportet a te baptizari; et, Ecce agnus Dei, hic est, qui tollit peccata mundi etc....Misit eos ad Christum in hunc finem ut miracula conspicati in fide ejus confirmarentur.

Traces of the influence of the passage may also be found in Isho'dad.

The passage is imitated by Bar-Hebraeus *in loc.*

ܠܘ ܕܠܐ ܝܕܥ ܗܘܐ
ܠܗ ܗܘ ܝܘܚܢܢ ... ܘܗܐ
ܡܩܕܡܘ ܣܗܕ ܩܕܡ ܟܢ̈ܫܐ
ܕܗܘܝܘ ܐܡܪܗ ܕܐܠܗܐ

. . . .

ܕܠܫܘܪ̈ܪ ܬܠܡܝܕܘܗܝ ܕܠܐ
ܡܗܝܡܢܝܢ ܗܘܘ ܫܕܪ ܐܢܘܢ
ܠܘܬܗ.

i.e. It was not that John did not know him...whereas he had already testified before the multitudes that he is the Lamb of God...to confirm his disciples who did not believe, he sent them to him.

Mösinger, p. 101.

Matt. xi. 7. *Quid existis videre in deserto? arundinem vento agitatum?* i.e. num Joannes timebat persecutores et ab omni vento flectebatur, ut aliquando diceret, 'Ecce agnus Dei' et postea nuncium ad eum mitteret, 'Tu es qui venturus es, an alium exspectamus?'

Isho'dad (f. 67 v.).

ܗܢܘ ܕܠܡܚܙܐ ܠܡ ܢܦܩܬܘܢ
ܠܡܕܒܪܐ ܠܡܚܙܐ. ܩܢܝܐ
ܕܡܢ ܪܘܚܐ ܡܬܬܙܝܥ....
ܕܒܕܡܘܬ ܩܢܝܐ ܕܡܢ ܪܘܚܐ
ܡܬܬܙܝܥ ܘܡܬܬܪܝܡ ܠܟܠ
ܓ̈ܒܝܢ. ܘܗܟܢ ܐܝܟ ܕܦܠܓܝܢ
ܗܘ ܒܫܘܐܠܬ ܕܡܫܬܐܠ
ܒܪ̈ܒܝܢܘܗܝ. ܘܗܟܢ ܐܡܪܐ
ܡܪܐ ܠܗ ܘܥܒ̄. ܘܗܟܢ

ܫܠܚ ܠܗ. ܕܐܢ ܐܢܬܘ

ܗܘ ܕܐܬܐ.

i.e. In the passage What went ye out into the wilderness to see? A reed shaken by the wind...A man who in the likeness of a reed shaken and bent to every side, and easily changed in his opinion by those who meet him; so that at one time he calls him 'the Lamb, etc.' and at another sends to him to know 'Art thou he that should come?'

Mösinger, p. 111.

Matt. xii. 32. Et quod dicit: Neque hic neque illic dimittetur ei, quia Dominus peccata multorum condonat et baptismus ejus poenam credentibus gratis dimittit.

Isho'dad, f. 198 v.

ܡܪܝ ܐܦܪܝܡ. ܠܐ

ܒܥܠܡܐ ܗܢܐ. ܥܠ ܕܫܒܩ

ܡܪܢ ܡܓܢ ܚܛ̈ܗܐ ܣܓܝܐܐ

ܘܐܦ ܒܡܥܡܘܕܝܬܐ ܫܒܩܗ̇

ܡܓܢ.

Mar Ephrem. Neither in this world; because our Lord freely remitted many sins, and also in baptism he remits it freely.

Mösinger, p. 112.

Aut de illo tempore quo in terra ambulavit, id dixit, non autem de futuro. Viderunt eum carne indutum et multi hac de causa de divinitate ejus dubitarunt, sed de Spiritu praejudicatae opiniones non erant

....

....

In his autem diebus ex inscientia blasphemant. Omnes ergo nati possunt ad poenitentiam pervenire, quare ei qui non potest poenitentiam agere, melius erat, si natus non fuisset. Omnibus per poenitentiam est remissio, sive scientes sive inscientes peccaverunt.

Isho'dad, f. 198 v.

ܘܙܕܩ ܕܢܕܥ. ܕܗܕܐ ܡܠܬܐ

ܥܠ ܙܒܢܐ ܗܘ ܐܬܐܡܪܬ ܘܠܐ

ܥܠ ܡܢܟܝܠ. ܚܙܐܘܗܝ ܓܝܪ

ܣܓ̈ܝܐܐ ܕܦܓܪܐ ܡܠܒܫ.

ܘܣܓ̈ܝܐܐ ܐܬܦܠܓܘ ܥܠܘܗܝ.

ܥܠ ܪܘܚܐ ܕܝܢ ܠܝܬ ܗܘܐ

ܠܗܘܢ ܠܡܣܒܪ ܡܕܡ.

ܡܓܕ̈ܦܢܐ ܕܝܢ ܕܡܘܡܢܐ

ܠܘ ܒܠܐ ܝܕܥܬܐ ܡܓܕܦܝܢ

ܘܕܫܪܒܐ.

ܠܟܠ ܕܝܠܝܕ¹ ܠܒܪ ܡܢ ܫܐܕܐ
ܕܬܗܘܐ ܬܝܒܘܬܐ ܒܟܠ
ܚܛܗܐ. ܕܒܝܕܥܬܐ ܘܒܠܐ
ܝܕܥܬܐ ܗܘܐ.

i.e. And we must know that this word is spoken concerning that time, and not of our day. For many saw him clad in a body, and many doubted concerning him; but concerning the Spirit they had no means of supposing anything. But the blasphemers of our own day do not blaspheme without knowledge, etc. Repentance is possible to every one that is born, and for every sin, whether in knowledge or in ignorance.

Mösinger, p. 113.

Ne putaveritis Deum non dimittere si poenitentiam agunt, tali enim blasphemia Satanas eos ad poenitentiam redire non permittit.

Isho'dad (f. 199 r.).

ܠܘ ܕܝܢ ܕܗܘ ܠܐ ܫܒܩ
ܠܗܘܢ ܐܢ ܬܝܒܝܢ. ܐܠܐ
ܕܒܗܕܐ ܓܘܕܦܐ ܠܐ ܫܒܩ
ܠܗܘܢ ܣܛܢܐ ܕܢܬܬܘܒܘܢ.

i.e. Not that he does not remit sin to them if they repent. But in this blasphemy Satan does not suffer them to repent.

Mösinger, p. 116.

Luke x. 18. *Videbam ego Satanam, quod decidit quasi fulmen de coelo,* non ac si in coelo fuisset..............

....

Non cecidit de coelis, quia et fulmen, quod a nube gignitur, de coelo cadere non potest. Cur ergo dixit: De coelis cecidit veluti fulmen? Quia subito ictu oculi Satanas victoriosae cruci subjectus est..............................

Sicut fulmen e loco suo egressum nunquam revertitur, ita et Satanas

Isho'dad (f. 196 v.).

ܚܙܝ ܐܦܪܝܡ. ܫܢܝܬܗ
ܠܣܛܢܐ ܕܢܦܠ ܐܝܟ ܒܪܩܐ:
ܠܘ ܡܢ ܫܡܝܐ ܢܦܠ. ܐܝܟ
ܒܪܩܐ ܕܝܢ ܡܢ ܥܢܢ ܘܒܚܕ
ܪܘܦܐ ܢܦܠ ܣܛܢܐ ܬܚܝܬ
ܙܩܝܦܗ ܕܙܟܝܐ. ܘܐܝܟ
ܕܒܪܩܐ ܢܦܩ ܘܠܐܬܪܗ ܠܐ

¹ Cod. ܕܝܠܕ

cecidit et in suum principatum nunquam restituetur.

ܗܦܟ. ܗܟܢܐ ܘܣܛܢܐ
ܢܦܠ ܡܢ ܫܘܠܛܢܗ. ܘܬܘܒ
ܠܐ ܩܐܡ.

i.e. Mar Ephrem. I saw Satan that he fell like lightning; he did not fall from heaven: for as the lightning suddenly and in the twinkling of the eye Satan fell under the victory of the Cross. And as lightning goes forth and does not return to its place so also Satan fell from his power and does not rise again.

Mösinger, p. 121.

Luke xi. 24. Porro dici potest, diabolum Israelem ad instar illius hominis possedisse et possidere. Quando in Aegypto habitabant et potestati Pharaonis subditi erant, ille immundus apud eos erat. Et quum Deus eis salvatorem misisset, qui eos educeret, ille immundus aufugit et sanati sunt. Misit verbum suum et sanavit et liberavit eos a perditione.

Isho'dad, f. 198 r.

ܐܡܪ ܓܝܪ ܡܪܝ ܐܦܪܝܡ.
ܕܪܘܚܐ ܠܡ ܒܝܫܬܐ ܕܥܡܪܐ ܗܘܬ
ܒܥܡܐ ܒܡܨܪܝܢ ܒܫܘܥܒܕܗܘܢ.
ܥܪܩܬ ܡܢܗܘܢ ܒܝܕ ܡܘܫܐ
ܦܪܘܩܗܘܢ. ܐܝܟ ܕܐܡܪ
ܕܘܝܕ. ܕܫܕܪ ܠܡ ܡܠܬܗ
ܘܐܣܝ ܐܢܘܢ. ܘܟܡ (l. ܘܟܕ)
ܕܐܬܟܪܟܬ ܗܘܬ ܗܦܟܬ
ܟܕ ܕܒܪܬ ܫܒܥ ܐܚܪ̈ܢܝܢ
ܪ̈ܘܚܝܢ ܕܒܝܫܢ ܡܢܗ.

For Mar Ephrem says: that the evil spirit which was in the people in Egypt in their subjection, fled away from them at the hand of Moses their Saviour. As also David said, He sent his word and healed them. And when it had gone about, it returned again taking seven other spirits worse than itself.

Mösinger, p. 121.

Luke xi. 24. Ille igitur *immundus* ex eis *expulsus* transivit *per loca arida* i.e. per gentes, ut inveniret requiem.

Bar-Hebraeus *in loc.*

ܒܐܬܪ̈ܘܬܐ. ܗ̄ ܒܥܡ̈ܡܐ ܚܢ̈ܦܐ.

In places, i.e. amongst the heathen peoples.

Mösinger, p. 122.

Luke xi. 24. Quaesivit et invenit sibi requiem in populo Israel.

Bar-Hebraeus *in loc.*

ܠܘܬ ܝܗ̈ܘܕܝܐ ܕܠܐ ܗܝܡܢܘ.

With the unbelieving Jews.

Mösinger, p. 122.

Luke xi. 26. Porro isti septem, qui in eo habitaverunt, illi sunt, de quibus Jeremias dixit: Concepit et peperit septem. Inflatus est venter ejus; peperit unum vitulum in deserto, duos vitulos Jeroboami et simulacrum quatuor facierum Manassis.

Isho'dad (f. 198 v.).

ܗܠܝܢ ܕܐܡܪ ܥܠܝܗܘܢ
ܐܪܡܝܐ. ܕܐܬܬ (l. ܕܐܠܬ)
ܠܡ ܝܠܕܬ ܫܒܥܐ. ܐܘܠܕܬ
ܓܝܪ ܥܓ̈ܠܐ ܒܡܕܒܪܐ
ܘܬܪܝܢ ܕܝܘܪܒܥܡ. ܨܠܡܐ
ܕܐܪܒܥܐ ܐܦ̈ܝܢ ܕܡܢܫܐ.

Those seven, namely, of which Jeremiah spoke: She conceived and brought forth seven: for she brought forth the calves, one in the desert and the two of Jeroboam, and the image of four faces of Manasseh.

Mösinger, p. 129.

Luke iv. 24. Non est propheta acceptus in patria. Non recepit Anathot Jeremiam, non Thesbi Eliam, non Abemahul Elisaeum, non Rama Samuelem, nec populus recepit Moysen, nec Israel Dominum.

Isho'dad (f. 188 v.).

ܐܝܟܢܐ ܕܠܐ ܡܩܒܠܐ
ܐܬܩܒܠ ܡܢ ܟܢܘܫܬܐ
ܥܡ ܪ̈ܒܘ ܐܬ̈ܘܬܐ ܕܥܒܕ
ܒܝܢܬܗܘܢ܆ ܘܠܐ ܫܡܘܐܝܠ
ܡܢ ܒܢ̈ܝ ܪܡܬܐ ܘܠܐ ܐܠܝܫܥ
ܡܢ ܒܢ̈ܝ ܡܚܘܠܐ. ܘܠܐ
ܐܪܡܝܐ ܡܢ ܒܢ̈ܝ ܥܢܬܘܬ.

i.e. As Moses was not accepted by the Congregation, with 10,000 miracles that he did amongst them; nor Samuel by the men of Rama, nor Elisha by the men of Mehola, nor Jeremiah by the men of Anaoth.

Mösinger, p. 134.

John vi. 12. *Colligite fragmenta coenae, ne quid ex eis pereat*, et ne credant, ad speciem tantum eum hoc fecisse. Cum enim fragmenta unum alterumve diem conservaverint, eis persuasum erit, Dominum hoc vere fecisse.

Isho'dad (f. 80 r.).

ܕܠܐ ܢܣܬܒܪ ܕܦܢܛܣܝܐ
ܕܚܪܫܐ ܐܬܚܫܚ ܐܠܐ
ܟܕ ܡܬܢܛܪ ܫܪܟܐ ܝܘܡܐ
ܘܬܪܝܢ ܕܢܗܝܡܢܘܢ ܕܫܪܝܪܐ
ܥܒܕ.

i.e. In order that it might not be supposed that he had made use of magical phantasy; but that, when the remainder had been kept for a day or two, they might believe that he had done it truly.

Mösinger, p. 140.

John iv. 5. Dominus noster quasi venator ad puteum venit.

The figure is a favourite one with Ephrem: cf. Serm. *De Dom. nostro* (ed. Lamy, i. p. 178).

ܨܝܕܐ ܗܘܐ ܕܢܚܘܬ ܕܢܨܘܕ
ܚ̈ܝܐ ܕܐܒܝ̈ܕܐ.

i.e. He became a hunter that he might descend and catch living men who had perished. Cf. also ed. Rom. iii. 396.

Isho'dad (f. 258 v.).

ܟܕ ܐܙܠܘ ܠܡܙܒܢ ܠܚܡܐ
ܥܠ ܕܨܒܐ ܗܘܐ ܕܢܨܘܕ
ܨܝܕܐ ܥܠ ܒܐܪܐ.

i.e. While they went away to buy bread, because he wished to go a hunting by the well.

Mösinger, p. 141.

John iv. Ab initio itaque colloquii personam suam ei non manifestam fecit, sed primo Judaeum, tunc prophetam et postremo Christum se ei revelavit. Per gradus ex ordine usque ad ultimum gradum eam deduxit. Primo enim vidit ut hominem sitientem, dein ut Judaeum, postea, ut prophetam, denique ut Deum. Homini sitienti persuadere voluit, a Judaeo abhorruit, doctorem interrogavit, a propheta correpta est, et Christum adoravit.

Isho'dad (f. 259 v.).

ܡܠܬ ܡܠܬ ܓܝܪ ܡܘܕܥ
ܢܦܫܗ ܠܫܡܪܝܬܐ. ܠܘܩܕܡ
ܟܕ ܨܗܝܐ. ܘܡܢ ܝܗܘܕܝܐ.
ܘܡܢ ܡܫܝܚܐ. ܡܢ ܕܪܓܐ
ܠܕܪܓܐ ܥܠ ܐܘܒܠܗ̇ ܥܠ
ܪܝܫ ܕܪܓܐ. ܒܡܕܪܫܐ ܫܪܝܬܗ
ܐܝܟ ܨܗܝܐ. ܘܡܢ ܝܗܘܕܝܐ.
ܘܡܢ ܢܒܝܐ ܘܡܢ ܐܠܗܐ.

ܐܠܐ ܐܦ ܗܝ ܐܝܟ ܕܠܨܗܝܐ
ܚܙܬ ܐܦܝܣܬܗ. ܘܐܝܟ ܕܡܢ
ܝܗܘܕܝܐ ܚܠܨܬ. ܘܐܝܟ
ܕܠܡܠܦܢܐ ܫܐܠܬ[1]. ܘܐܝܟ
ܕܡܢ ܢܒܝܐ ܐܬܟܣܬ. ܘܐܝܟ
ܕܠܡܫܝܚܐ ܣܓܕܬ.

Little by little he revealed himself to the Samaritan woman; first by his thirst, and then as a Jew, and then as the Christ; from degree to degree he led her and set her on the highest degree. She saw him first as a thirsty man, then as a Jew, then as a prophet, and then as God. And also it is she who would have persuaded him as a thirsty man, who would have shrunk[2] as from a Jew, and she asked questions as from a doctor, and was reproved as by the prophet, and worshipped him as God.

Mösinger, p. 141.

John iv. 42. Quum haec miracula vidissent et mirabilem et stupendam revelationem mulieri Samaritanae factam audiissent, occasionem irrisionis Judaeis praeripuerunt, qui dicturi erant, in professione mulieris adulterae fidem eorum esse fundatam. Propterea mulieri dixerunt: *Non postmodum propter verba tua credimus in eum, sed quia audivimus nos doctrinam ejus et vidimus opera ejus, quia Deus est, et cognovimus, eum profecto esse Christum verum.* Etenim super scientia nostra fundamenta fidei nostri poni oportuit.

Isho'dad, f. 259 v.

ܘܫܪܘ ܬܕܡܘܪܬܐ ܘܓܠܝܢܐ
ܕܫܡܥܘ ܡܢ ܗܝ ܐܢܬܬܐ
ܦܘܩܘܩܗ̇ ܠܒܠܥܬܐ ܕܠܐ
ܬܗܘܐ ܠܗ ܘܠܗܘܢ ܚܣܕܐ
[ܗܢ][3] ܡܘܕܝܐ ܕܟܠ ܟܠܢܫ
ܠܡ ܕܓܝܪܬܐ ܡܣܬܒܪܐ
ܫܬܐܣܬܐ ܕܗܝܡܢܘܬܗܘܢ.
ܘܟܠ ܗܕܐ ܐܡܪܘ ܠܗ̇.
ܕܠܘ ܡܛܠ ܡܠܬܟܝ ܡܗܝܡܢܝܢ
ܒܗ. ܚܢܢ ܓܝܪ ܫܡܥܢܢ
ܡܠܦܢܘܬܗ ܘܚܙܝܢ ܘܚܕܝܢ

[1] Cod. ܬܫܐܠܬ [2] Lit. shewn her teeth. [3] Cod. om.

ܠܓܠܝܢܘܬܗ. ܕܗܘܐ ܡܣܒܪܢܐ
ܙܢܝܬܐ. ܘܐܦ ܟܐܢܐ
ܗܝ ܠܢ ܕܝܕܥܬܢ ܬܗܘܐ
ܫܬܐܣܬܐ ܠܗܝܡܢܘܬܢ.

i.e. And they saw the marvels and revelations which were too great for the woman, and they cut off the occasion that there might not be a reproach upon Him and them from the Jews that you have set the foundations of your faith on the revelation of an adulteress. And on this account they said to her, Not for thy word do we believe in him, for we have heard his teaching and we know and see his might, that he is the true Christ. And moreover it is right that our knowledge be the foundation of our faith.

Mösinger, p. 147.

Si enim res creatae, angeli et luminaria et ros et pluvia et fontes et flumina die sabbati non cohibentur; si die sabbati nec angeli removentur a suo servitio et famulatu, nec coeli a mittendis roribus et pluviis, nec luminaria a cursu, nec terra a proferendo fructu, nec homo a respiratione et generatione, immo potius die sabbati homines generantur.

Imitated by Isho'dad, f. 263 r.

ܫܒܩ ܐܢܐ ܠܢ ܟܘܪܟܐ
ܕܫܡܫܐ. ܡܫܒܐ ܕܪ̈ܘܚܐ.
ܪܗܛܐ ܕܢܗܝܪܘܬܐ. ܦܓܘܕܬܐ
ܕܝ̈ܡܡܐ. ܡܚܬܬܐ ܕܡܛܪܐ.
ܡܦܩܐ ܕܥܝ̈ܢܐ ܡܘܠܕܐ
ܐܒܝܫ ܘܬܪܒܝܬܐ ܕܒܢܝ̈ܢܫܐ
ܘܕܟܠ ܫܢ̈ܝܢ. ܡܕܒܪܢܘܬܐ
ܕܝܢ ܟܠ. ܗܠܝܢ ܕܒܐܪ̈ܥܐ
ܕܡܠܐ̈ܟܐ ܡܬܓܥܪܝܢ.
ܐܝܟ ܓܒܝܢܗ.

i.e. For I leave on one side the circuit of the sun, the blast of the winds, the course of the luminaries, the bridling of the seas, the descent of the rain, the casting out of devils, the birth and bringing up of men and of all living things, and providence towards everything, those things which are perfected by the hand of angels according to his will.

Mösinger, p. 156.

Matt. xvii. 3. Sive mortui sunt ut Moyses, resurgent, sive vivunt, ut Elias, ad eum volabunt.

Isho'dad, f. 87 r.

ܡܘܫܐ ܕܝܢ ܡܢ ܡܝ̈ܬܐ.
ܘܐܠܝܐ ܡܢ ܚܝ̈ܐ.

Moses from the dead, and Elias from the living.

Bar-Hebraeus *in loc.*

ܘܐܬܚܙܝ ܠܗܘܢ ܡܘܫܐ
ܗ̄ ܡܢ ܡܝ̈ܬܐ. ܘܐܠܝܐ
ܗ̄. ܡܢ ܚܝܐ.

And there appeared to them Moses (i.e. from the dead) and Elias (i.e. from the living).

The Maronite Breviary (ed. 1665) repeatedly plays on the same string: e.g. (Feast of Transfiguration).

ܐܬܬܚܙܝ ܠܡܘܫܐ ܡܢ
ܒܝܬ ܡܝ̈ܬܐ. ܘܐܦ ܠܐܠܝܐ
ܡܢ ܒܝܬ ܚܝ̈ܐ.
ܐܬܘ ܠܣܝܥܬܗܘܢ ܡܢ ܡܝ̈ܬܐ
ܐܦ ܡܢ ܚܝ̈ܐ.
ܠܡܘܫܐ ܢܣܒ ܡܢ ܡܝ̈ܬܐ
ܘܠܐܠܝܐ ܡܢ ܒܝܬ ܚܝ̈ܐ
ܕܫܠܝܛ ܥܠ ܡܝ̈ܬܐ ܘܥܠ
ܚܝ̈ܐ.

etc. etc.

Mösinger, p. 156.

Matt. xvii. 4. *Si vis, Domine, faciamus hic tria tabernacula.* Quod dixit, quia illum montem a vexationibus Scribarum vacuum et quietum vidit et hoc ei placuit.

Bar-Hebraeus *in loc.*

ܘܢܦܠܛ ܡܢ ܪܘܒܐ ܕܝܗ̈ܘܕܝܐ.

i.e. And we shall escape from the tumult of the Jews.

Mösinger, p. 156.

Luke ix. 33. *Nesciebat quod diceret,* quia Dominus crucem erat ascensurus, vel quia tabernacula non hic eis concessa erant, sed in mundo venturo. Facite, ait, vobis amicos, qui vos recipiant in tabernacula aeterna.

Isho'dad, f. 193 r.

ܠܐ ܝܕܥ. ܗܘܐ ܕܚܫܬ.
ܕܚܫ ܡܪܢ ܘܢܙܕܩܦ. . . .
ܬܘܒ. ܕܠܐ ܝܕܥ ܗܘܐ
ܕܡ̈ܛܠܠܐ ܠܘ ܬܡܢ ܐܢ̈ܝܢ.
ܐܠܐ ܒܥܠܡ ܢܘܗܪܐ ܒܗܝ
ܕܡ̈ܛܠܠܐ ܕܐܦܝܣ ܫܡܥܘܢ.
ܬܡܢ ܐܦܢ ܢܩܒܠܘܢܟܘܢ
ܠܡ ܒܡ̈ܛܠܠܝܗܘܢ ܕܠܥܠܡ.

i.e. He did not know that our Lord was about to suffer and be crucified. ...Again he did not know that the tabernacles are not there, but in the world of light; and the passage referring to the tabernacles that Peter persuaded him to make, is 'there they shall receive you indeed in their tabernacles for ever.'

Mösinger, p. 163.

Luke xv. 7. Cur autem gaudium est de peccatoribus, qui poenitentiam agunt, magis quam de justis, qui non peccarunt. Quia gaudium esse solet post tristitiam. Quoniam ergo tristitia est eis qui peccarunt, gaudium fiat, quando agunt poenitentiam.

Isho'dad, f. 205 v.

ܘܡܬܒܥܝܐ ܕܠܡܘܢ
ܗܘܐ ܚܕܘܬܐ ܥܠ ܚܛܝ̈ܐ
[ܬܘܒ][1] ܕܬܝܒܝܢ ܝܬܝܪ ܡܢ ܕܥܠ
ܙܕܝ̈ܩܐ ܕܠܐ ܚܛܘ. ܘܐܡܪܝܢ
ܚܕܐ ܕܚܕܘܬܐ ܕܒܬܪ
ܟܪܝܘܬܐ ܗܘܐ ܘܐܢ ܟܪܝܘ[2]

[1] Repeated *ex errore.*

[2] Cod. ܘܐܕܟܪܝܘ (*sic*).

Luke xv. 11—29. Note that the Armenian commentary shews only three lines on the Prodigal Son, ending with a significant, etc. Some of the missing matter is probably in the long comment of Isho'dad on the parable, but we have no means of identifying it.

ܟܕ ܚܛܘ. ܚܕܝܢ ܗܫܐ
ܒܬܝܒܘܬܗܘܢ.

And the enquiry is made Why is their joy over sinners that repent more than over the righteous that have not sinned? And we say that it is joy that is after pain, and if they were pained when they sinned, now they rejoice over their turning.

Mösinger, p. 165.

Luke xiii. 1. *Et factum est, ut venientes ei narrarent de Galilaeis, quorum sanguinem Pilatus miscuit cum sacrificiis eorum*, scilicet in festivitate regni Herodis, quo tempore gladio amputavit caput Johannis. Nimirum quia Joannes injuste et contra legem occisus est, Pilatus exercitum collegit et mittens perdidit omnes, qui simul aderant in illo convivio. Et quia Herodes aliud facere nequibat, propter ignominiam ipsi illatam occidit omnes praefectos exercitus Pilati, eique iratus est usque ad diem judicii Domini, qui causa erat reconciliationis eorum. Pilatus miscuit sanguinem eorum cum sacrificiis eorum, quia illi arcebantur a potestate Romanorum, ne holocausta et sacrificia possent offerre. Novit Pilatus, eos legem transgressos esse, et holocausta et sacrificia obtulisse, quare in illo loco eo tempore eos occidit.

Isho'dad (f. 80 r.).

ܦܝܠܛܘܣ ܕܝܢ ܫܡܥ
ܥܘܠܐ ܕܐܣܬܥܪ ܒܝܘܚܢܢ.
ܫܕܪ ܩܛܠ ܠܟܠܗܘܢ ܠܡܙ̈ܡܢܐ
ܕܬܡܢ ܗܘܘ. ܘܡܢ ܗܘ
ܝܘܡܐ ܗܘܬ ܒܥܠܕܒܒܘܬܐ
ܒܝܢ̈ܬܐ. ܘܒܝܘܡ ܚܫܗ
ܕܗܘ ܡܫܝܢܢܐ ܕܟܠ. ܗܘܘ
ܪ̈ܚܡܐ ܥܡ ܚܕܕܐ ܗܪܘܕܣ
ܘܦܝܠܛܘܣ.

i.e. But Pilate heard of the wickedness done to John, and sent and killed all the guests that were there; and from that day there was enmity between them. And in the day of the suffering of him, the reconciler of all, Pilate and Herod became friends with one another.

Isho'dad (f. 201 v.).

ܗܘ ܕܐܬܘ ܐܢܫܝܢ ܘܐܡܪܘ
ܠܗ ܥܠ ܓܠܝܠܝ̈ܐ. ܗܢܘܢ
ܕܦܝܠܛܘܣ ܚܠܛ ܕܡܗܘܢ
ܥܡ ܕܒ̈ܚܝܗܘܢ. ܡܛܠ
ܕܒܪ ܕܟܠܝܢ ܗܘܘ ܡܢ ܫܘܠܛܢܐ

ܕܗ̈ܘܡܢܝܐ ܕܠܐ ܢܕܒܚܘܢ.
ܟܕ ܐܫܟܚ[1] ܐܢܘܢ ܦܝܠܛܘܤ
ܕܥܒܪܘ[2] ܥܠ ܦܘܩܕܢܐ ܘܕܒܚܘ
ܠܫܐ̈ܕܐ. ܚܪܒܗ ܐܢܘܢ
ܒܗ̇ ܒܕܘܟܬܐ ܘܒܗ ܒܥܕܢܐ
ܕܕܒܚܘ. ܘܚܠܛܘ ܟܐܡܬ
ܥܡ ܕܒ̈ܚܐ ܐܦ ܕܡܐ
ܕܕܒܘ̈ܚܐ.

It says: There came men who told him of the Galileans whose blood Pilate had mingled with their sacrifices. For because they were restrained by the authority of the Romans from sacrificing, when Pilate found that they had transgressed the command and sacrificed to devils, they put them to the sword in the very place and at the very time that they had sacrificed, and thus they mingled with the sacrifices the blood of the sacrificers.

Isho'dad (f. 228 r.).

ܡܪܝ ܐܦܪܝܡ. ܒܥܠܕܐ
ܕܒܥܬ ܠܗܘ ܕܗܘܪܘܤ ܟܕ
ܫܡܥ ܕܡܪܝ ܡܫܝܚ ܐܬܦܫܩ
ܕܠܐ ܒܝܕܗܘܤ. ܫܕܪ ܦܝܠܛܘܤ
ܗ̈ܘܡܢܝܐ ܘܩܛܠ ܠܐܝܠܝܢ
ܕܐܫܬܟܚܘ ܒܡܫܡܫܐ
ܟܕ ܐܫܟܚ[1] ܐܢܘܢ ܟܐܡܬ
ܕܡܕܒܚܝܢ ܒܗ ܟܠܗܝܢ ܡܢ
ܗ̈ܘܡܢܝܐ ܕܠܐ ܢܕܒܚܘܢ
ܘܪܘܚܘ ܥܠ ܚܕܐ ܡܢ ܗܘ

[1] Cod. ܐܫܟܚܘ [2] Cod. ܕܥܒܪ

ܣܘܟܐ. ܐܬܪܥܘ ܕܝܢ
ܒܝܘܡ ܚܫܗ ܕܥܠܬ[1] ܫܝܢܐ
ܕܟܠ ܒܪ̈ܝܢ.

Mar Ephrem. At the birthday feast of Herod, when the head of S. John was cut off unlawfully, Pilate sent Romans and killed those who had taken part in the banquet, for he found out that they were sacrificing, though forbidden to sacrifice by the Romans. And they were enraged with one another from that day; but they were reconciled on the day of the suffering of him who is the cause of the peace of all created things.

Mösinger, p. 166.

Voluerunt enim comperire, utrum strages eorum propter ipsorum sacrificia ei placeret, sicque contra legem et cum gentilibus esset, an sacrificium defenderet, quo casu eum apud Pilatum accusaturi erant, quod imperio Romanorum adversaretur.

Isho'dad (f. 201 v.).

ܗܠܝܢ ܕܝܢ ܕܐܬܘ ܐܝܟ
ܕܠܡܢܣܝܘܬܗ ܐܫܬܕܪܘ.
ܕܢܕܥܘܢ ܡܢܐ ܐܡܪ. ܕܐܢ
ܢܐܡܪ ܕܙܕܩܐܝܬ ܐܬܩܛܠܘ
ܢܫܬܟܚ ܣܩܘܒܠ ܢܡܘܣܐ.
ܘܐܢ ܒܝܫܐܝܬ ܐܡܪ ܥܠ
ܩܛܠܗܘܢ ܢܐܟܠܘܢ ܩܪ̈ܨܘܗܝ
ܩܕܡ ܦܝܠܛܘܣ. ܕܠܩܘܒܠ
ܡܠܟܘܬܐ ܗܘ ܕܪ̈ܗܘܡܝܐ.

Those who came were sent for the purpose of tempting him, that they might know what he would say. And if he should say that they were righteously killed, he would be found to be an adversary of the law; but if he speak evilly of their murder, they would accuse him before Pilate as being adverse to the kingdom of the Romans.

[1] Cod. ܥܠܬ.

Mösinger, p. 166.

Luke xiii. 6. *Alia parabola: Homo quidam plantaverat in vinea sua ficum et dicit ad colonum.* Colonus hic erat lex, ad legem enim respexit. *Hi tres anni sunt, quod venio quaerere fructus ex hac ficu,* quod propter tres captivitates dixit, quibus Israelitae captivi ducti et castigati, non autem emendati sunt.

Isho'dad (f. 202 r.).

ܐܚܪ̈ܢܐ ܗܕܐ ܠܗ
ܦܠܐܬܐ. ܥܠ ܙܒܢܐ
ܕܬܝܒܘܬܐ ܐܡܪܗ̇. ܬܐܬܐ
ܥܡܐ. ܦܠܚܐ ܢܡܘܣܐ.
ܬܠܬܐ ܫܢܝ̈ܢ ܕܫܒܝܗܘܢ
ܐܫܬܒܝܘ ܐܝܟ ܕܢܬܪܨܘܢ
ܘܠܐ ܐܬܬܪܨܘ.

Others say, that in this parable he spake of the time of repentance. The fig-tree is the people; the gardener, the law; [the three years] the three captivities in which they were led captive that they might be reformed, but they were not reformed.

Mösinger, p. 166.

Luke xiii. 8. *Dimitte eam et hoc anno.* Annuit Dominus se fore longanimem erga eos, quod est tempus septuaginta hebdomadum.

Isho'dad (f. 202 r.).

ܗܝ ܕܫܒܘܩܝܗ̇ ܐܦ ܗܕܐ
ܫܢܬܐ. ܗ̄. ܙܒܢܐ ܕܫܒܥܝܢ
ܫܒ̈ܘܥܝܢ.

The words 'Let it alone this year also' intimate the time of seventy weeks.

Mösinger, p. 167.

John vii. 3. Quoniam eum tradere voluerunt, propterea eos fefellit dicens, Non ascendo.

Isho'dad (f. 268 r.).

ܡܪܝ ܐܦܪܝܡ ܟܐܠ ܠܗܘܢ
ܕܐܦ ܐܚܘ̈ܗܝ ܠܗ ܨܒܘ
ܬܡܢ ܕܢܫܠܡܘܢܝܗܝ. ܒܡܘܚܪܐ
ܓܝܪ ܕܣܘܠܩܗ ܠܥܐܕܐ....

Mar Ephrem blames them, because even his brethren wished there to betray him; for by the delay of his going up to the feast, &c.

Mösinger, p. 174.

Matt. xix. 16. Et quomodo renunciavit huic nomini is qui de se ipso dixit; Pastor bonus animam suam dat pro ovibus suis...? Porro: Qui seminavit semen frumenti sancti ipse est filius hominis et semen bonorum filii sunt regni. Quomodo semen potest esse bonum, et qui id seminat malus?

Isho'dad (f. 96 r.).

ܘܠܢܦܫܗ ܕܐܢܐ ܐܢܐ
ܪܥܝܐ ܛܒܐ. ܘܗܘ ܠܗ
ܕܙܪܥ ܙܪܥܐ ܛܒܐ ܐܬܘܗܝ
ܒܪܗ ܕܐܢܫܐ. ܘܐܝܟܢ
ܡܫܟܚܐ ܕܙܪܥܐ ܢܗܘܐ
ܛܒܐ ܘܙܪܘܥܗ ܒܝܫܐ.

He said of himself, that I am the good shepherd; and he that sowed the good seed is the Son of man, and how is it possible that the seed should be good and its sower bad?

Mösinger, p. 175.

Luke xvi. 22. At cur solum Abrahamum, non autem ceteros justos vidit, *et Lazarum in sinu ejus?*

Isho'dad (f. 214 r.).

ܠܐܒܪܗܡ ܕܝܢ ܐܕܟܪ
ܒܡܬܠܐ ܘܠܐ ܠܕܘܝܕ
ܘܠܫܪܟܐ.

He commemorates Abraham in the parable, and not David and the rest.

Mösinger, p. 180.

Luke xix. 5. Precabatur Zachaeus in corde suo et dixit: Beatus est quicunque dignus invenietur, ut in domum ejus iste justus intret. Et dixit ei Dominus: *Festina, descende istinc, Zachaee!* Qui cum intellexisset, Dominum cogitationem ejus novisse, dixit: Si istam cogitationem novit, omnia quoque quae unquam feci, scit. Ideo respondit '*Omnia quae unquam ab aliquo injuste accepi, reddam haec quadruplum.*'

Isho'dad (f. 219 r.).

ܟܕ ܡܨܠܐ ܒܪܥܝܢܗ.
ܛܘܒܘܗܝ ܠܟܠ ܕܫܘܐ
ܕܢܥܘܠ ܗܢܐ ܙܕܝܩܐ ܠܒܝܬܗ.
ܡܪܢ ܕܝܢ ܝܕܥ ܘܐܡܪ ܠܗ.
ܐܣܬܪܗܒ ܚܘܬ ܙܟܝ. ܘܗܘ
ܟܕ ܚܙܐ ܕܝܕܥ ܠܪܥܝܢܗ
ܐܟܚܕ ܘܠܡܫܟܚܗ ܐܡܪ.
ܐܝܟܢܐ ܕܗܘܐ ܝܕܥ ܟܠ
ܕܥܒܕܬ ܝܕܥ ܘܟܠ ܗܕܐ
ܐܡܪ ܕܟܠ ܕܥܠܒܬ ܚܕ
ܒܐܪܒܥܐ ܦܪܥܢܐ.

i.e. While he was praying inwardly [and saying] Blessed is every one who is worthy that this righteous man should enter into his house. And our Lord knew it and said to him, Make haste and come down, Zacchaeus. And he, when he saw that he knew him, both his name and his thought, said, 'This man, if he knows this, knows everything that I have done'; and therefore he said 'Whatever I have defrauded, I repay fourfold.'

Mösinger, p. 151.

Matt. xxi. 12. Quas autem intra templum oves et boves vendebant, eae erant quas sacerdotes ex sacrificiis colligebant.

Isho'dad (f. 102 v.).

In this passage, concerning those sheep and oxen, &c., that were sold there, they were those which were offered to God and the priests sold them again, as Mar Ephrem witnesses.

Mösinger, p. 182.

Matt. xxi. 19. Similiter Gergesaei consilium ceperunt, non egrediendi ad Dominum, quare porcos eorum suffocavit, ut excitarentur et vel inviti ad eum exirent.

Ita et possessor hujus ficulneae decreverat, Christum non adire, et hic arefecit ficulneam ejus, ut invitus ad ipsum veniret, quia Dominus in omnibus occasionibus salutem hominum desiderabat.

Isho'dad (f. 105 v.).

Rursus quando dixit, Destruite templum hoc, et tertia die suscitabo illud, ei responderunt, Quadraginta sex annis, &c....Itaque ad monstrandam potestatem divinitatis suae maledixit ficulneae et arefacta est.

Cf. Mösinger, p. 44.

Nemo ex urbe Gergesenorum ad ipsum exire voluit, donec ibi miraculum faceret.

Also, Mösinger, p. 75.

Gergeseni consilium ceperant, neque exeundi, neque videndi signum Domini. Ideo suffocavit gregem porcorum eorum, ut inviti exirent.

i.e. Others say, that just as the Gadarenes had made an agreement not to go out to Jesus, and on this account he choked their pigs, in order that they might come out though unwillingly; so the lord of the fig-tree had made up his mind not to come out to him, and therefore he made his fig-tree to wither. For by all means he wished to save men.

Others say, that because when our Lord said of the temple of his body that in three days I will raise it up; and of the temple of stones that there shall not be left, &c., there was a doubt of his word, by the miracle of the drying up of the fig-tree it confirmed his word.

¹ Cod. om. ܠܟ.

Mösinger, p. 184.

Matt. xxi. 21. Iterum dicunt, quod ait, *Dicetis huic monti*, non est mons, sed diabolus, aut simile aliquid.

Bar-Hebraeus *in loc.*

ܠܛܘܪܐ ܗܢܐ ܬܐܡܪܘܢ
... ܠܣܛܢܐ.

Ye shall say to this mountain, i.e. to Satan.

Cf. in Matt. xvii. 20,

ܠܛܘܪܐ ܠܣܛܢܐ ܩܪܐ.

He called Satan the mountain.

Cf. Isho'dad (f. 89 v).

ܠܛܘܪܐ ܡܫܝܚܐ ܡܪܢ
ܒܡܬܠܐܝܬ ܠܚܝܠܘܬܗ
ܕܣܛܢܐ.

Our Lord parabolically calls the powers of Satan 'mountain.'

Mösinger, p. 185.

Matt. xxi. 21. Si iste mons daemon erat, ut illi opinantur, de eo id quoque valeret, quod sequitur: *mittere in mare*. Verum qua ex causa si quis daemonem ejecit, in mare eum mittet? at fortasse haec eis erit causa, quod Dominus [hac ratione] daemones ejecit?

Bar-Hebraeus *in loc.*

ܐܝܟܢܐ ܕܓܕܫ ܠܕܝܘܐ
ܕܥܠܘ ܒܚܙܝܪܐ.

i.e. according as it happened to the devils who entered into the swine.

Mösinger, p. 186.

Sed quum tempus suae passionis prope esset, ne quis putaret eum comprehensum esse, quia se ipsum liberare non posset, Dominus ficulneae maledixit......praeveniens, per inanimatam plantam quam arefecit, ostendit se per verbum etiam crucifixores suos perdere posse.

Bar-Heb. in Matt. xxi.

ܐܠܐ ܕܢܕܥܘܢ ܬܠܡܝܕܐ
ܚܝܠܗ ܕܒܨܒܝܢܗ ܚܐܫ ܘܐܠܘ
ܨܒܐ ܐܝܟ ܕܠܬܬܐ ܐܘܒܫ
ܘܐܡܝܬ ܠܨܠܘܒܐ.

i.e. that his disciples might know his power, that he suffers of his own will, and that if he had willed, just as he made the fig-tree wither he would have put to death the crucifiers.

And cf. Isho'dad (f. 104 v.).

Mösinger, p. 186.

Admirati sunt discipuli ejus, quomodo tam subito arefacta sit. Quia nempe sua natura ficus, si caeditur, propter viriditatis abundantiam post multos demum menses arida fit.

Isho'dad (f. 105 r.).

ܘܡܢ ܐܝܠܢܐ ܕܡܢ ܟܠ
ܪܟܐ ܘܪܛܒ. ܗܘ ܕܐܦ
ܡܬܦܣܩ ܠܡܝܒܫ ܒܢܘܪܐ
ܒܥܣܩ. ܘܠܗܢܐ ܒܡܦܩܢܘܬܗ̇
ܕܡܠܬܐ ܐܘܒܫ.

And from a tree which of all trees is moist and green, so that even when it is cut down it is with difficulty dried by fire; and this tree he dried up by the utterance of his word.

Mösinger, p. 192.

Matt. xxi. 33. *Et sepe munivit eam*, nempe lege, *et torcular praeparavit* in ea, altare, *et aedificavit in ea turrim*, templum, etc.

Isho'dad (f. 106 r.).

ܣܝܓܐ ܕܝܢ ܠܢܛܘܪܘܬܐ
ܕܐܬܝܗܒܬ ܠܗܘܢ ܡܢ
ܒܥܘܕܪܢܐ ܐܠܗܝܐ....
ܡܥܨܪܬܐ ܠܡܕܒܚܐ
ܕܒܣ̈ܡܐ....

The fence [he calls] the observance that was given to them by the Divine aid...the tower, the temple; the wine-vat, the altar of incense, &c.

Moses Bar-Kepha (f. 98, b. 1).

ܦܘܫܩܐ ܕܡܬܠܐ.
ܡܫܡܥܬ. ܟܪܡܐ ܗܘܐ
ܠܐܠܗܐ ܘܟܪܡܐ ܠܥܡܐ.
ܣܝܓܐ ܠܢܛܘܪܘܬܐ ܕܢܡܘ̈ܣܐ.
ܐܘ ܠܥܘܕܪܢܐ ܕܡܢ ܐܠܗܐ.
ܡܓܕܠܐ ܗܝܟܠܐ.
ܘܡܥܨܪܬܐ ܟܠܬܐ ܗܘ
ܕܥܠܘܗܝ ܡܬܐܣܪ ܗܘܐ ܕܡܐ
ܕܕܒ̈ܚܐ. ܦܠܓ̈ܐ ܕܝܢ ܬܟܠܬܐ

ܕܦܘ̈ܫܩܐ. ܒܒ̈ܪܐ ܕܐܬܦܪܫܘ
ܘܪܐ ܠܢܡ̈ܘܣܐ. ܬܛܪܕܬܐ
ܕܐܝܟ ܕܒܣܪܬܐ ܕܒܪܗ.
ܠܡܐܬܝܬܗ ܕܠܗ ܡܫܝܚܐ.
ܕܐܦܩܘܗܝ ܕܐܝܟ ܠܒܪ ܡܢ
ܟܪܡܐ ܘܩܛܠܘܗܝ ܕܐܝܟ
ܕܡܢܗܘܢ ܐܒܝܕ ܗܘܐ.

Exposition of Matthew succinctly.

He calls God the man, and his people the vineyard; the hedge is the observance of laws, or the help of God; the tower is the temple, the wine-vat is the altar on which the blood of the sacrifices is shed; the husbandmen are the band of priests; the servants that were sent are the prophets; the sending of the son at the last he calls his own coming; and that they cast him out of the vineyard and killed him means that he perished at their hands.

Bar-Hebraeus *in loc.*

ܣܝܓܐ ܗ. ܣܡ ܠܗ
ܢܡܘܣܐ ܘܚܦܪ ܒܗ
ܡܥܨܪܬܐ ܗ̄ ܡܕܒܚܐ
ܕܕܒ̈ܚܐ.

The fence, i.e. he established the law; and digged a wine-vat in it; i.e. the altar of sacrifices.

Mösinger, p. 193.

Matt. xxi. 42. *Lapis quem reprobaverunt aedificantes, ipse factus est caput anguli.* Qualis lapis? Is qui dicitur adamantinus his verbis: Pono ego adamantem in medio filiorum Israel.... Et dictum est "Super quem cadet," &c.

Isho'dad (f. 106 v.).

Whosoever shall fall on the stone of adamant.

ܡܢ ܕܢܦܠ ܥܠ ܟܐܦܐ
ܕܐܕܡܘܣ.

The influence of Ephrem on Isho'dad is perceptible, though slight. Note that Mösinger again fails to identify the quotation from the Old Testament. It is Amos vii. 8.

ܗܐ ܐܢܐ ܣܐܡ ܐܢܐ
ܐܕܡܘܦ ܒܓܘ ܥܡܝ
ܐܝܣܪܝܠ.

Mösinger, p. 197.

John viii. 48. Samaritanum autem Dominum vocarunt, quia Samaritani de se ipsis contra Judaeos affirmant: Nos sumus filii Abrahae, ut et Judaei contra eos idem de se contendunt. Quum jam Dominus ad Judaeos dixisset: *Si filii estis Abrahae, etiam opera ejus facite,* Judaeis visum est, partes Samaritanorum hoc ejus verbum tueri, ideo dixerunt ad eum, Samaritanus es tu.

Isho'dad (f. 273 v.).

ܦܪܐܘܗܝ ܫܡܪܝܐ ܡܛܠ
ܕܫܡܪ̈ܝܐ ܥܠ ܢܦܫܗܘܢ
ܠܘܩܒܠ ܝܗܘ̈ܕܝܐ ܐܡܪ̈ܝܢ
ܕܚܢܢ ܐܝܬܝܢ ܒܢ̈ܝ ܐܒܪܗܡ.
ܘܝܗܘ̈ܕܝܐ ܠܘܩܒܠܗܘܢ
ܕܚܢܢ ܐܝܬܝܢ ܒܢ̈ܝ ܐܒܪܗܡ.
ܘܟܕ ܫܡܥܘ ܡܪܢ ܕܐܡܪ
ܒܢ̈ܝ ܐܒܪܗܡ [ܗܘܝܬܘܢ]
ܥܒ̈ܕܘܗܝ ܕܐܒܪܗܡ ܥܒܕܝܢ
ܗܘܝܬܘܢ. ܣܒܪܘ ܕܠܓܒܐ
ܕܫܡܪ̈ܝܐ ܡܠܬܐ ܩܝܡܐ.
ܟܕ ܐܣܟܡܐ ܕܝܗܘ̈ܕܝܐ
ܠܒܝܫ.

They called him a Samaritan because the Samaritans say of themselves against the Jews that 'we are the children of Abraham,' and the Jews say the same against the Samaritans. And when they heard our Lord saying 'If ye would be the children of Abraham, do the works of Abraham,' they supposed that the Word stood on the side of the Samaritans, though he was clad in the form of the Jews.

Mösinger, p. 197.

John viii. 56. *Abraham desideravit videre diem meum, vidit et gavisus est.* Quem diem? Illum, de quo ei dictum est: 'In semine tuo benedicentur omnes gentes.' Vidit autem et gavisus est quia vidit mysterium agni.

The mystery of the lamb seen by Abraham is the 'ram caught in the thicket.' Cf. Mösinger, p. 207, Vidit Abraham diem meum et gavisus est, nimirum per agnum in arbore qui solvit et liberavit Isaac ligatum, ut et Dominus vincula gentium solvit per crucem.

Imitated by Isho'dad (f. 274 r.).

ܝܘܡܗ. ܗ. ܠܗܘ
ܕܙܩܝܦܐ. ܠܗܘ ܕܒܗ ܚܠܦ
ܚܝܐ ܕܟܠ ܩܒܠ ܡܘܬܐ.

His day: i.e. the day of the Cross: on which he accepted death for the life of all.

Mösinger, p. 198.

John ix. 6. Et fecit lutum ex sputo suo, et fecit oculos in hoc luto.

. . . .

Non enim Siloe solvit oculos caeci, ut nec aquae Jordanis Naaman sanarunt, sed mandatum Christi hoc effecit.

Imitated by Isho'dad (f. 305 r.).

ܒܪܘܩܐ ܕܡܢ ܦܘܡܗ
ܐܬܓܒܠ ܥܝܢ̈ܐ. ܘܡܢ ܒܡܝ̈ܐ
ܕܫܝܠܘܚܐ ܐܬܦܩܕ ܕܢܣܚܐ
ܐܕܝܢ. ܘܐܠܘ ܒܟܣܝܘܬ ܠܐ
ܐܬܓܒܠ ܗܘ̈ܝ. ܐܦܢ ܣܚܐ
ܡܣܓܝ ܗܘܐ ܠܗ ܒܫܝܠܘܚܐ
ܠܐ ܡܘܬܪܐ ܗܘܬ. ܐܝܟ
ܕܐܦܠܐ ܢܥܡܢ ܡܬܕܟܐ
ܡܢ ܓܪܒܗ ܒܡܝ̈ܐ ܕܝܘܪܕܢ
ܐܠܘ ܚܝܠܐ ܐܠܗܝܐ ܠܐ
ܡܕܟܝܐ ܗܘܬ ܠܗ ܒܝܕ
ܐܠܝܫܥ.

By the spittle from his mouth the eyes were fashioned, and then he was commanded to wash in the waters of Siloam: but unless the eyes had secretly been fashioned, he might have washed in Siloam many times without advantage; even as Naaman would not have been cleansed from his leprosy by the waters of Jordan unless the Divine power had cleansed him by the hand of Elisha.

Mosinger, p. 200.

John x. 8. Quod ait: Omnes qui ante me venerunt, fures erant et latrones; de Theuda et Juda dixit.

Isho'dad (f. 277 v.).

ܐܢܫ ܕܝܢ ܬܐܘܦܘܪܘܣ
ܗܟܢ ܦܫܩ. ܓܢܒܐ ܐܝܬܘܗܝ
ܡܛܥܝܢܐ ܘܕܓܠܐ ܐܝܟ
ܬܐܘܕܐ ܘܝܗܘܕܐ ܘܕܫܪܟܐ.

i.e. a God-possessed man interprets it on this wise: the thief is the deceiver and the liar, like Theudas and Judas, &c.

The interpretation was shown by Zahn (*Tatian*, p. 47) to exist in the margin of copies of the Heraclean version at John x. 8 in the form 'Theudas, Judas the Galilean &c.' But here Ephrem does not seem to be named. Isho'dad does not name Ephrem, but speaks of the interpretation being due to a 'Theophorus,' a form of quotation which he sometimes employs.

The interpretation, however, is certainly popular with the author of the Commentary, for we find (i) that he returns to it on p. 209 'Et illis annis surrexit Theodas ejusque socii quos Christus latrones vocavit'; (ii) the verse commented on was a favourite Marcionite proof-text, and was sure to require special treatment in such an anti-Marcionite book as the Commentary undoubtedly is. Note that Isho'dad (f. 278 v.) is sensible of its bearing on the Marcionite controversy, for he says

ܠܘ ܓܝܪ ܠܡܘܫܐ ܘܠܓܘܕܐ ܕܢܒܝ̈ܐ ܩܪܐ ܓܢܒ̈ܐ
ܘܓܝܣ̈ܐ ܐܝܟ ܦܟܝܗܘܬܐ ܕܡܪܩܝܘܢ ܘܡܐܢܝ.

i.e. He does not call Moses and the choir of the prophets thieves and robbers, according to the foolishness of Marcion and Mani.

Mösinger, p. 200.

John xi. 4. Compara jam verbo Vivificatoris et intellige quomodo inter se conveniant. Ad caecum dixit: *Non hujus est peccatum nec cognatorum ejus, sed ut revelentur opera Dei in isto:* et de morbo Lazari dixit: *Hic morbus non est ad mortem sed*

Isho'dad (f. 281 r.).

ܗܝ ܕܢܫܬܒܚ ܒܪܗ
ܕܐܢܫܐ ܡܛܠܬܗ. ܕܣܡܝܐ
ܠܗܝ ܕܡܛܠ ܚܛܗܐ ܐܡܪ.
ܕܠܐ ܗܘܐ ܘܠܐ ܐܒܗ̈ܘܗܝ

propter gloriam Dei ut glorificetur in eo Filius Dei.

ܐܠܐ ܕܢܬܚܙܘܢ ܒܗ
ܥܒ̈ܕܘܗܝ ܕܐܠܗܐ.

The passage 'that the Son of man may be glorified in him,' is similar to what he said in the case of the blind man, 'neither this man nor his parents, but that the works of God may be seen in him.'

Mösinger, p. 201.

John xi. 9. Quibus verbis per comparationem et imaginem Apostolos voluit docere, Judaeos ante finem anni remissionis, qui est mater mensium, non esse offensuros per occisionem Domini, qua tenebrae regnaturae erant in Sion. *Nonne duodecim horae sunt diei?* i.e. quid timetis, ne lapidemini? Donec ego vobiscum sum, nemo vestrum mecum et pro me patietur; verum venient super vos tenebrae, plenae doloribus, quando a vobis elevatus ero et vos dimittam. Sed accipietis coronas, ut et ego, qui coronabor et e medio vestrum elevabor.

Isho'dad (f. 282 r.).

ܐܚܪ̈ܢܐ. ܨܒܐ ܠܡ
ܒܦܠܐܬܐ ܗܕܐ ܕܢܠܦ
ܠܬܠܡ̈ܝܕܐ ܕܩܕܡܐ ܕܫܘܠܡܐ
ܫܢܬܐ ܕܫܘܒܩܢܐ ܕܐܝܬܝܗ̇
ܐܡܐ ܕܝܪ̈ܚܐ ܠܐ ܡܬܬܩܠܝܢ
ܡܘ̈ܗܕܢܐ ܒܩܛܠܗ.
ܗܘ ܕܡܡܠܟܝܢ[2] ܚܫܘܟܐ[1]
ܒܨܗܝܘܢ.
ܐܚܪ̈ܢܐ. ܕܫܠܝܬܘܢ ܠܡ
ܡܢ ܕܐܢܐ ܒܗ ܥܡܟܘܢ
ܐܢܐ. ܐܢܫ ܡܢܟܘܢ ܥܡܝ
ܘܚܠܦ ܠܐ ܡܐܟܬ. ܡܕܝܢ
ܠܟܘܢ ܓܝܪ ܚܫܘܟܐ ܡܠܐ
ܚܫܬܐ[3] ܘܡܪܝܪܘܬܐ ܘܟܦܢܐ
ܟܕ ܐܬܥܠܐ ܡܢܟܘܢ
ܘܐܫܒܘܩܟܘܢ ܕܬܣܒܘܢ
ܡܫܠܡܬܘܢ. ܘܬܣܒܘܢ
ܟܠܝ̈ܠܐ ܘܕܘܒܪ̈ܐ.

i.e. others interpret: He wished by this parable to teach his disciples

[1] Cod. ܚܫܘܟܐ. [2] Cod. ܘܡܡܠܟܝܢ. [3] Cod. ܚܫܘܟܐ.

that until the year of his gospel was completed, which is the mother of months, the Jews will not be offended at his murder, [in which month] darkness will reign in Zion.

Others say: Are you afraid of the people while I am with you? None of you will die with me or instead of me. For darkness will come upon you full of suffering and sickness and fear, when I shall be lifted up from you and shall make some of you to be offended in order that you may know your own weakness; and ye shall receive crowns, &c.

Mösinger, p. 201.

John xi. 15. Gavisus est quum audivit, flevit quum advenit. Dixerat, eum mortuum esse, antequam advenisset, et post adventum interrogavit 'Ubi posuistis eum?'

Isho'dad (f. 284 r.).

ܚܕܝ ܟܕ ܫܡܥ ܕܟܪܝܗ.
ܘܒܟܐ ܟܕ ܐܬܐ ܕܢܚܝܘܗܝ.
ܒܕܩ ܕܡܝܬ ܠܗ ܟܕ ܠܐ
ܒܕܠܐ ܠܡܐܬܐ ܘܫܐܠ
ܕܐܝܟܐ ܣܡܬܘܢܝܗܝ.

He rejoiced when he heard that he was sick and wept when he came to revive him; he comprehended that he was dead, before he came, and asked 'where have ye put him?'

Mösinger, p. 203.

John xi. 33. Quod autem *turbatus*, consonat cum eo quod dixit: *Quamdiu vobiscum ero, et vobiscum loquar?* et alio loco, Taedet me de generatione ista.

Isho'dad (f. 283 r.).

ܗܝ ܕܐܬܬܙܝܙ ܒܪܘܚܗ.
ܒܘܙܙܗ ܕܐܝܟ ܐܬܐ ܗܘ
ܕܣܡܝܟܬܐ ܥܠ ܡܗ̈ܘܕܝܐ
. . . .
ܕܡܢܟܐ ܠܘܬܪ ܗܕܐ ܠܗܝ
ܕܥܠ ܡܗܘܕܝܐ. ܘܐܬܒܙܙ
ܠܡ ܘܐܡܪ. ܕܢܣܝܒܘܢ ܠܡ
ܡܥܠܡ ܠܢ. ܘܠܗܝ ܕܒܢܡܐ

ܠܐܡܬܝ ܐܗܘܐ ܥܡܟܘܢ
ܐܘ ܠܘܬܟܘܢ ܘܐܣܝܒܪܟܘܢ
ܘܫܪܟܐ.

The expression, 'He was angered in his spirit' [implies that] his perturbation was a sign of his anger over the Jews.... It is like to the passage concerning Judas, that he was angered and said that 'one of you will betray me'; or to this 'How long shall I be with you and suffer you, &c.?'

Mösinger, p. 204.

John xi. 39. *Accedite et auferte lapidem.* Qui mortuum vivificavit et vitam in eum redemit, nonne et potuit aperire sepulcrum et auferre lapidem? Qui discipulis suis dixerat, Si habetis fidem ut granum sinapis, dicetis monti huic: Transferre et transferretur a facie vestra, nonne hic lapidem ab ore sepulcri potuit removere? Profecto, qui in cruce pendens voce sua petram et sepulcra scidit, potuit et verbo suo lapidem istum levare. Sed quia Lazarus amicus ejus erat, dixit: Aperite vos ipsi, ut odor foetoris ejus nares eorum tangeret, et *solvite eum* vos ipsi ab eis quibus eum ligastis, ut opus manuum vestrarum cognoscatis.

Ideo tempore mortis Lazari Dominus ad hunc pagum se non contulit, ne dicerent: Pactum inter se constituerunt.

Isho'dad (f. 284 r.).

ܗܘ ܕܐܚܝܐ ܡܝܬܐ ܘܐܦܝܣ
ܢܦܫܐ ܘܫܪܟܐ. ܠܐ ܡܨܐ
ܗܘܐ ܡܒܪܐ ܠܡܦܬܚ
ܘܟܐܦܐ ܠܡܥܓܠܘ ܒܥܠܬܐ.
ܘܗܘ ܕܐܡܪ ܠܬܠܡܝܕܘܗܝ
ܕܐܢ ܬܗܘܐ ܒܟܘܢ
ܗܝܡܢܘܬܐ ܐܝܟ ܦܪܕܬܐ
ܕܚܪܕܠܐ ܬܐܡܪܘܢ ܠܛܘܪܐ.
ܘܗܘ ܕܒܩܠܗ ܒܙܩܝܦܐ
ܟܐ̈ܦܐ ܘܩܒܪ̈ܐ ܨܪܝ
ܘܫܪ̈ܟܐ. ܐܝܠܐ ܡܥܓܠ
ܕܪܚܡܗ ܗܘܐ ܕܠܥܙܪ. ܐܡܪ
ܕܦܬܚܘ ܡܒܪܐ ܕܢܡܛܐ
ܪܝܚܐ ܕܣܪܝܘܬܐ
ܒܐܦ̈ܝܗܘܢ ܘܐܫܬܪܝܘܗܝ
ܐܢܬܘܢ. ܕܐܠܨܬܘܢܝܗܝ
ܕܬܫܬܘܕܥܘܢ ܥܒܕ
ܐܝܕܝܟܘܢ

ܘܟܠ ܗܕܐ ܒܕ ܡܟܐܬ
ܠܐ ܫܡܫܠ ܢܦܫܗ ܬܡܢ
ܕܠܐ ܢܐܡܪܘܢ ܕܐܬܢܘ
ܫܘܫ ܒܝܢܬܗܘܢ.

i.e. He who quickened the dead and brought back the soul, &c.: was not he able to open the grave and to roll away the stone by a word? And he who said to his disciples, If ye had faith as a grain of mustard, ye should remove mountains; and he who by his voice on the cross shattered rocks and graves, &c.: But because he was the friend of Lazarus he said 'Open the grave,' in order that the smell of his putrefaction might reach their nostrils, and 'Loose him,' ye who clad him, in order that ye may recognize the work of your hands.

On this account, when he died, he did not present himself there, that it might not be said that they had made an agreement between them.

Mösinger, p. 213.

Matt. xxiv. 15. Romani intra templum vexilla sua statuerunt, in quibus erat figura aquilae.

Isho'dad (f. 112 r.).

ܡܪܝ ܐܦܪܝܡ. ܗܘ ܕܝܢ
ܕܣܝܡܘܗ ܠܗܝ [ܗ̄. ܒܢܕܐ]
ܕܨܝܪ ܒܗܘܢ ܢܫܪܐ ܫܩ ܥܠ
ܪܘܡܚܐ ܘܐܥܠ ܠܗܝܟܠܐ.

Mar Ephrem: this means that he set the standards, on which was represented an eagle, on the top of a spear and brought them into the temple.

[The word 'standard' is explained by Isho'dad by an alternative term.]

Mösinger, p. 213.

Matt. xxiv. 15. Alii dicunt, signum dirutionis ejus fuisse quod Romani caput porci apportandum et per Pilatum intra templum collocandum curarunt.

In both the Armenian and the Syriac this extract follows immediately on the preceding.

Isho'dad (f. 112 r.).

ܐܚ̈ܪܢܐ ܕܝܢ ܐܡܪܝ ܕܠ
ܕܚܙܝܪܐ ܐܝܬܝ ܦܝܠܛܘܣ.

Others say that Pilate brought in the head of a pig.

Mösinger, p. 214.

Matt. xxiv. 20. *Orate et petite, ne sit fuga vestra in hieme, nec in die sabbati,* videlicet, ne in captivitate abducamini, quo tempore non licet operari. Ut hiems sine fructibus est, et sabbatum sine operatione, ita cavete, ne vos abducamini, quando nec fructum habebitis nec operationem.

Isho'dad (f. 225 v.).

That they may not be taken in the winter nor on the sabbath: either it refers to the end of the world, or the separation of every soul from the body: since 'winter' implies defect of fruit, but 'the sabbath' vacancy from labours: that is, pray that you may not be taken when you have no time for labour and when you are deprived of the fruits of faith and of works of virtue.

Mösinger, p. 214.

Ne forsitan, ait, si innocentes et simplices in vobis inveniantur, ita sabbatum tempore belli observent, sicuti pactum foederis observare debetis, neve vos occidant, sicuti eos qui in illo antro occisi sunt.

Isho'dad (f. 225 v.).

ܘܠܐ ܒܫܒܬܐ. ܟܕ
ܒܛܠܝܬܘܢ܆ ܕܠܡܐ ܟܕ
ܢܫܬܟܚܘܢ ܒܟܘܢ ܦܫܝ̈ܛܐ[1]
ܘܦܘ̈ܪܫܐ ܠܡܛܪ ܫܒܬܐ
ܒܙܒܢܐ ܕܩܪܒܐ ܢܚܒܠܘܢ
ܐܢܘܢ ܐܝܟ ܗܢܘܢ
ܕܒܡܥܪܬܐ.

i.e. *And not on the Sabbath;* when ye are idle; lest when there shall be found among you simple people and intent on keeping the Sabbath, in time of war they should destroy them as they did those who were in the cave.
(Cf. 1 Macc. ii. 31—38.)

Mösinger, p. 215.

Luke xxi. 36. *Orate ut digni sitis eximi ab his omnibus quae ventura sunt.* Haec quoque, ut nonnulli explicant, de punitione urbi Jerusalem instante Dominus dixit, iisdemque verbis finem mundi significavit.

Isho'dad (f. 225 r.).

ܬܫܬܘܐܝܬ ܗܢ ܗܝ
ܕܗܢ ܒܗܘ ܠܒܝܬ ܠܝܗܘ̈ܕܝܐ.
ܡܬܚܠܠܐܝܬ ܕܝܢ ܗܝ
ܕܒܫܘܠܡܗ ܕܥܠܡܐ. ܡܛܠ
ܕܐܦ ܡܠܘ̈ܗܝ ܕܡܪܢ ܗܪܟܐ
ܥܠ ܬܪ̈ܝܗܘܢ ܙܒ̈ܢܐ
ܡܠܦܝܢ.

Historically the passage implies what has already happened to the Jews: metaphorically, what will happen in the end of the world. Because, moreover, the words of our Lord in this place teach concerning both times.

Mösinger, p. 215.

Luke xxi. 36. Alii dicunt, ad solos Apostolos haec dicta esse, ut, si feria sexta sol defecturus sit, conforta-

Isho'dad (f. 225 v.).

ܐܚܪ̈ܢܐ. ܕܠܘܬ ܫܠܝ̈ܚܐ
ܠܚܘܕ ܐܬܐܡܪܬ. ܥܪܘܒܬܐ.

[1] Cod. ܒܫܝ̈ܛܐ (sic).

rentur. Porro ait, In Sabbato, quia
de Sabbato Judaei jactabantur; et,
In hieme, quia frigida est.

Some people say, that it was spoken
only of the Apostles. The Sabbath,
because on the night of the Sabbath
(sic!) they were apprehended and ran
away. And winter, because it was
cold. (Cf. John xviii. 18.)

Mösinger, p. 216.

Matt. xxiv. 36. *Diem illum nemo
scit, neque Angeli, neque Filius*, ut
illud; Discedite a me maledicti Patris
mei in ignem aeternum, quia non novi
vos. Sicut ergo novit malos, sed
propter eorum opera dicit: Non novi
vos: ita etsi momentum adventus
sui novisset etc.

Imitated in
Isho'dad (f. 163 r.).

If the words 'He knows not the
day,' and this passage 'I knew you
not,' which he spake over the foolish
virgins, and 'I never knew you' which
he said to the leaders of heresies,
must be understood as of outward
familiarity, &c.

Mösinger, p. 216.

Matt. xxiv. 36. Quomodo jam momentum adventus sui non novit? Si
Patrem novit, quid, quaeso, Patre
majus est, quod nesciret?

Isho'dad (f. 115 v.).

And he does not know the day.
Then that day is something greater
than the Father.

6—2

Mösinger, p. 217.

Matt. xxiv. Porro scriptum est: Consilium Dei Christus est, per quem revelata sunt omnia occulta sapientiae et scientiae.

Isho'dad (f. 162 v.).

ܘܐܠܐ ܐܝܟܢ ܐܡܪ ܫܠܝܚܐ
ܕܒܗ ܟܣܝܢ ܟܠܗܘܢ ܣܝܡܬܐ
ܕܚܟܡܬܐ ܘܕܝܕܥܬܐ.

Otherwise how did the Apostle say that 'in Him are hid all the treasures of wisdom and knowledge'?

Mösinger, p. 217.

Matt. xxiv. 36. Et Spiritus ea quae ab ipso condita sunt, novit, ut et illi affirmant, quia profunda Dei scrutatur, Filius autem haec nesciat.

Isho'dad (f. 115 v.).

ܘܐܢ ܪܘܚܐ ܠܟܠܡܕܡ
ܒܨܝܐ. ܐܦ ܠܥܘ̈ܡܩܘܗܝ
ܕܐܠܗܐ. ܪܘܚܐ ܕܝܢ ܕܝܠܗ
ܕܡܫܝܚܐ ܘܐܝܟܢ ܠܐ ܗܠܝܢ
ܕܒܐܝ̈ܕܘܗܝ...

And if the Spirit searches all things, even the depths of God, and the Spirit is Christ's own, how is it that He does not know those things which are done by His hands?

Mösinger, p. 221.

John xiii. 26. *Et intinxit eum*, ut sic participationem indicaret caedis suae plene patratae, qua corpus sanguine ipsius intinctum est. Aut ideo intinxit panem, ne cum pane etiam testamentum daret. Lavavit prius panem et tunc illum ei dedit.

Controverted by Isho'dad (f. 164 v.).

ܗܝ ܕܝܢ ܕܐܡܪܝܢ. ܕܨܒܥ
ܝܫܘܥ ܠܠܚܡܐ ܘܝܗܒ
ܠܗ. ܘܚܦ ܩܕܝܫܘܬܐ ܘܚܦ
ܒܘܪܟܬܐ ܕܒܪ̇ܟ ܐܫܟܚܗ.
ܠܝܬ ܠܗ ܕܘܡܝܐ.

As to what some say, that Jesus dipped the bread and gave it to him, and washed off its sanctity and the blessing which he had invoked, there is no likelihood in it.

It appears that Ephrem is really concerned over the fact that Judas had partaken of the holy bread and presumably inherited eternal life thereby; so he invents a theory of the de-consecration of the elements, by dipping the bread in water. (Cf. Maher, *Diatessaron.*) Isho'dad very properly rejects the theory.

It appears, however, in Moses bar Kepha, with a special reference to the Commentary of Ephrem.

Moses bar Kepha (f. 115 b. 2).

ܐܝܟ ܡܪܝ ܝܥܩܘܒ ܕܝܢ ܐܡܪ ܐܦ ܡܪܝ ܐܦܪܝܡ
ܒܦܘܫܩܐ ܕܐܘܢܓܠܝܘܢ̈ ܝܗܘܕܐ ܕܝܢ ܠܠܚܡܐ ܕܨܒܥ
ܡܪܢ ܘܝܗܒ ܠܗ ܢܣܒܗ ܠܗܘ ܠܚܡܐ ܘܐܙܠ ܨܝܕ
ܟܗܢ̈ܐ ..... ܐܫܝܓܗ ܡܪܢ ܘܥܒܕܗ ܕܠܐ ܩܘܕܫܐ.

i.e. Mar Ephrem in his Commentary on the Gospels says the same as Mar Jacob. Judas took the bread, that bread which the Lord dipped and gave him, and went to the priests....Our Lord washed it and made it unconsecrated.

Mösinger, p. 221.

Matt. xxvi. 26. Ex illo momento, quo discipulis suis corpus suum fregit, et corpus (l. sanguinem) suum Apostolis dedit, numerantur tres dies ejus, quibus cum mortuis computabatur, ut et Adam, qui, postquam de illa arbore comedit, multis annis vixit, quamvis propter mandati transgressionem mortuis annumeratur, quia Deus ita dixit, Quo die comederis, morieris.

Isho'dad (f. 71 r.).

ܐܢܫ̈ܐ. ܡܢ ܙܒܢܐ ܠܗ
ܕܩܨܐ ܗܘܐ ܦܓܪܗ. ܘܡܙܓ
ܕܡܐ. ܒܗܝ ܕܡܢ ܗܘ
ܙܒܢܐ ܚܫܝܒ ܗܘܐ ܡܪܢ
. . . . ܡܢ ܗܝ
ܕܨܝܕ ܐܕܡ ܕܒܝܘܡܐ
ܕܬܐܟܘܠ ܡܢ ܐܝܠܢܐ
ܡܡܬ ܬܡܘܬ. ܘܗܘ ܚܝ̈ܐ
ܬܫܥܡܐ̈ܐ ܘܬܠܬܝܢ ܫܢܝܢ.

Some say: from the time that he had broken his body and mingled the blood; for from that time our Lord was reckoned [among the dead]....

As in the word to Adam, that in the day that thou shalt eat of the tree, thou shalt surely die; and then his life was 930 years.

Mösinger, p. 222.

Matt. xxvi. 29. In posterum non bibam ex hoc genimine vitis usque ad regnum Patris mei...usque ad resurrectionem meam. Quod docet Simon in Actibus Apostolorum dicens: Post resurrectionem per quadraginta dierum tempus edimus cum eo et bibimus.

Isho'dad (f. 128 r.).

ܘܠܡܢܐ ܗܪܟܐ ܐܡܪ ܕܠܐ
ܐܫܬܐ ܡܢ ܗܫܐ. ܒܬܪ
ܩܝܡܬܗ ܕܝܢ ܕܐܟܠ ܥܡܗܘܢ
ܐܡܝܪܐ . . . .
ܬܘܒ ܕܒܬܪܬܝܗܘܢ ܐܬܚܫܚ
ܡܢ ܗܝ ܕܐܡܪ ܦܛܪܘܣ.
ܕܐܟܠܢ ܠܗ ܥܡܗ ܘܐܫܬܝܢ
ܒܬܪ ܩܝܡܬܗ.

And why does he here say 'I will not henceforth drink': but after his resurrection it is said that he ate with them...?

Again that he made use of both of these is clear from what Peter said 'We did eat with him and drink after his resurrection.'

Mösinger, p. 225.

John xiv. 16. Alium paraclitum mitto ad vos: i.e. consolatorem.

Isho'dad (f. 295 v.).

ܗܝ ܕܐܚܪܢܐ ܦܪܩܠܛܐ
ܗ. ܐܚܪܢܐ ܡܒܝܐܢܐ.

This expression 'another Paraclete' means 'another Comforter.'

Mösinger, p. 228.

John xvii. 5. *Clarifica Filium tuum et Filius clarificabit te.* Quod non quasi indigens, ut haec acciperet, rogavit, sed ordinem primarium creationis perfecturus postulavit gloriam etc.

Isho'dad (f. 306 r.).

ܘܐܠܐ ܐܢ ܣܢܝܩ ܗܘܐ
ܕܢܣܒ ܕܢܬܓܡܪ ܠܡܢܐ
ܟܕ ܐܝܬܘܗܝ....

And unless he were in need of receiving in order that he might be made perfect, why, since he is &c.

Mösinger, p. 231.

Matt. xxvi. 41. Quomodo Dominus, cujus auxilio Apostoli mortem suam despexerunt juxta verbum ejus: Nolite

Imitated by Isho'dad (f. 129 v.).

ܐܝܟ ܕܢܦܠ ܡܢ ܡܘܬܐ
ܡܕܡ ܕܝܢ ܗܘ ܡܢ ܢܦܫܐ.

timere eos, qui occidunt corpus, animam autem occidere non possunt: quomodo, dico, ipse mortem potuit timere?

ܠܐ ܠܡ ܬܕܚܠܘܢ ܡܢ
ܐܝܠܝܢ ܕܩܛܠܝܢ ܦܓܪܐ
ܘܕܚܪܢܐ.

If He feared death, then He was deficient in soul: Do not fear them that kill the body &c.

Mösinger, p. 239.

Matt. xxvii. 29. *Et in corona ex spinis*...quia Dominus per suam coronam sustulit maledicta Adae primi; 'Spinas et tribulos tibi germinabit.'

Isho'dad (f. 134 v.).

ܒܟܘܒܐ ܕܝܢ. ܠܒܘܛܠܗ̇
ܕܠܘܛܬܐ ܕܠܘܬ ܐܕܡ. ܠܝܛܐ
ܗܝ ܠܡ ܐܪܥܐ ܒܛܠܠܟ.
ܟܘܒܐ ܘܕܪܕܪܐ ܬܘܒܐ
ܠܟ.

And by the thorns [is intended] the abolition of the curse upon Adam; for 'Cursed is the ground for thy sake: thorns and briers shall it bring forth to thee.'

Mösinger, p. 239.

Dederunt arundinem in manu ejus .... Et sicut arundine confirmantur et ratae fiunt sententiae judicum, ita et Dominus per arundinem scripsit et ejecit e domo sua.

The influence of this curious conceit that the reed in Christ's hand was a writing reed may be seen also in Ephrem's Hymn on the Crucifixion (Lamy, i. 665).

Imitated by Isho'dad (f. 134 v.).

ܐܪܙܐ ܕܒܗ ܡܬܒܛܠ
ܫܛܪܐ ܕܐܬܟܬܒ ܥܠܝܢ ܒܝܕ ܐܕܡ.

An intimation that by it was cancelled the instrument that was written against us by the hand of Adam.

ܛܘܒܝܟ ܐܦ ܠܟ ܩܢܝܐ ܕܒܙܚܐ
ܕܠܟ ܢܩܦܬ ܗܘܬ ܐܝܕܗ ܕܡܠܟܢ
ܩܢܝܐ ܗܘ ܕܐܘܫܛܘܗܝ ܫܩܠܬܐ ܒܙܚܐ
ܕܐܝܟ ܕܝܢܐ ܟܬܒ ܘܫܪܐ ܐܘܦܝ

i.e. Blessings on thee also, thou reed of scorn,
In that to thee clave the hand of our king,

> The reed which fools made him hold for a type,
> Who like a judge wrote, and released them.

It has also influenced the later commentators; Bar-Ṣalibi says that 'by this scepter our Lord would cancel the Instrument of obligation which was written against us by Adam.' The coincidence with Isho'dad is exact.

Mösinger, p. 237.

Matt. xxvi. 65. Mense Arech, flores sinus suos rumpunt et egrediuntur, sinibusque suis nudis et inanibus relictis ipsi aliorum corona fiunt. Sic quoque mense Arech summus sacerdos sacerdotium dirupit et nudum et inane reliquit, et sacerdotium transiit et in Salvatore nostro collatum est.

Ephrem, *Hymn. in Resurr.* (ed. Lamy, ii. 762).

[Syriac text — eight lines]

In Nisan the flowers burst their cups
(lit. bosoms)
And their roses come forth;
They leave their cups in nakedness
And become a crown for others:
As is Nisan, so is its feast.
On the feast the high priest rent his
garments (*lit.* sinus)
And the priesthood fled from him,
And left him naked
And was spread over our Saviour.

As was pointed out above (p. 8), we have here an actual piece of Ephrem's poetry disguised as prose. The Armenian translator has misunderstood some points or abbreviated his text. He was perhaps puzzled with the expression 'as is Nisan, so is its feast,' and consequently 'sic quoque mense Nisan' has become attached to the next sentence.

Mösinger, p. 242.

Luke xxiii. 31. *Si in ligno viridi hoc faciunt.* Per comparationem Dominus 'lignum viride' suam divinitatem et 'lignum aridum' eos appellavit, qui dona ejus acceperunt.

....

Aut 'lignum viride' dixit, quia miracula fecit, et 'lignum aridum' justos vocat, quia facta mirabilia non fecerunt.

Isho'dad (f. 228 r.).

ܡܪܝ ܐܦܪܝܡ. ܠܪܛܝܒܐ
ܥܠ ܚܝܠܐ ܕܐܠܗܘܬܗ
ܦܫܩ. ܠܝܒܝܫܐ ܕܝܢ
ܠܬܠܡܝܕܘܗܝ.

. . . .

ܐܘ ܪܛܝܒܐ ܡܛܠ
ܬܕܡܪ̈ܬܐ ܕܥܒܕ. ܝܒܝܫܐ
ܕܝܢ ܐܝܠܐ ܕܡܢ ܗܕܐ
ܚܠܝ.

Mar Ephrem interprets the green wood of the power of his Divinity, but the dry wood of his disciples...or the green wood on account of the miracles which he did; the dry wood is the one who is destitute of this.

Mösinger, p. 245.

John xix. 23. Tunica ejus non est scissa, quae imago est divinitatis ejus, quae non dividitur, quia non est composita. Quod vestimentum ejus divisum est in quatuor partes, significat Evangelium in quatuor partes mundi egressurum.

Isho'dad (f. 310 v.).

ܡܪܝ ܐܦܪܝܡ. ܟܘܬܝܢܗ
ܠܡ ܕܠܐ ܐܬܨܪܬ ܐܪܙ
ܐܠܗܘܬܗ ܕܠܐ ܡܬܨܪܝܐ
ܘܠܐ ܡܬܦܠܓܐ. ܘܐܣܛܠܗ
ܕܠܐܪܒܥ ܡ̈ܢܘܢ ܐܬܦܠܓܬ
ܐܪܙ ܦܘܠܓܐ ܕܦܓܪܗ
ܘܛܘܦܣܐ ܕܣܒܪܬܗ
ܕܠܐܪܒܥ ܦܢ̈ܝܢ.

Mar Ephrem: The tunic which was not rent signifies his divinity, which is neither rent nor divided: and the robe that is divided into four parts signifies the division of his body and is a type of his Gospel which [goes] to the four quarters (Matt. xxviii. 19; Mark xvi. 15, 20): [or was it 'which is composed of four faces'?]

Mösinger, p. 257.

Aut quia typi viderunt agnum typicum, sciderunt velum et stipati egressi sunt ad eum aut spiritus prophetiae habitans in templo, qui descenderat ut hominibus adventum ejus praedicaret, tunc avolando ascendit, etc.

Imitated by Isho'dad (f. 136 v.).

ܐܦ̈ܝ ܬܪܥܐ ܕܐܬܦܬܚܘܢ
ܗܘܐ ܛܘܦܣܐ ܕܐܫܬܪܝ.
ܚܕܐ ܒܕܠܐ ܣܝܒܪ ܚܫܐ
ܕܪܫ[1] ܠܛܘܦܣܗ. ܘܬܪܬܝܢ
ܠܡܘܕܥܘ ܕܫܢܝܬ ܡܢܗ
ܫܟܝܢܬܐ ܐܠܗܝܬܐ
ܘܠܛܝܒܘܬܐ ܕܪܘܚܐ
ܕܩܘܕܫܐ.

The veil of the temple was rent; which was a type that was annulled; first, because it could not bear the suffering of its archetype; second, to shew that the Divine Shekinah had withdrawn from it and the grace of the Holy Spirit.

Mösinger, p. 266.

Matt. xxvii. 66. Obsignarunt sepulcrum ejus, quod pro Christo et contra eos accidit, ut in Daniele et Lazaro. Quum in lacu Danielis sigillum suum viderent, cognoscere poterant, qualis potentia liberaverat eum....

[Ephrem makes the same comparison with Daniel in his *Sermo ad Noct. Dom. Resurr.* (Lamy, vol. i. p. 530).

ܕܓܒܐ ܗܘܐ ܩܒܪܗ ܕܝܫܘܥ ܠܓܘܒܗ ܕܕܢܝܐܝܠ
ܕܐܬܚܒܫ ܗܘܐ ܘܚܬܝܡ ܦܘܡܗ.

i.e. The grave of Jesus was like the pit of Daniel which was closed and its mouth sealed.]

Corpus suum ex sepulcro signato eduxit et sigillum sepulcri testis fiebat sigillo uteri quem obsignaverat.

[Which figure will also be found in the sermon just quoted:

ܗܟܢܐ ܒܪ ܩܡ ܘܩܒܪܐ
ܩܒܪܐ ܚܬܝܡ ܘܐܬܚܬܡ.
ܠܐ ܫܪܐ ܠܒ̈ܬܘܠܘܬܐ ܕܡܒܪܗ:

Imitated by Bar-Ṣalibi.

'As he arose from the Virgin's womb without breaking the seals and virginity of her who bore him; so from his own virgin tomb did he

[1] Cod. ܪܫ

ܪܠܵܘܬ݂ܐ ܐܠ݂ܝ ܝܝܟ
ܕ݁ܝܠܵܬ݂ܗ.

i.e. As our Lord Jesus rose and
came forth and was raised, without
destroying the seals of his tomb: so
he did not destroy the virginity of
her that bare him.]¹

arise, the marks, seals and stones
entire and inviolate.' (Loftus, p. 50.)

And by Isho'dad (f. 138 r.).

ܘܗܘ ܒܗܪܐ ܘܡܬ݂ܐ ܐܬ݂ܠܪ
ܘܨܘܐ ܗܕ ܗܕ ܐܠ ܐܬ݂ܝܕܘ
ܠܘܬ݂ܐ. ܘܡܬ݂ܐ ܡܢ ܗܕ݂ܝܪ.
ܗܡܠ ܡܢ ܪܚܡ ܗܕ ܠܝܝܗ
ܐܪܐܬ݂ ܐܣܪ ܪܘܚܕܐ.

And in this first birth he was born
and came forth without dissolving
her virginity: and in this second
birth he came forth from the tomb,
the seals and stones being kept intact
together.

¹ The parallel between the womb and the tomb is a favourite one with the
Fathers: it appears in English literature in G. Herbert's lines.

> Thou hadst a virgin womb
> And tomb;
> A Joseph did betroth
> Them both.

CONCLUDING REMARKS.

The foregoing collection of agreements between the Commentary ascribed to Ephrem and the works of later Syriac Commentators will be sufficient to finally dissipate any residual scepticism as to the substantial authorship of the famous Commentary and as to the text upon which it is based. No one who is the least versed in *Quellen-Kritik* would have any doubt as to the dependence of the later Syriac commentators upon the Ephrem Commentary, even if they had transcribed their extracts without the frequent introductory formula that ' Mar Ephrem says.' Nor would any one who was acquainted with the writings of the great Syrian father fail to recognise that the Commentary (even if it had come down to us anonymously) was so full of Ephrem's ideas, and of extracts from his hymns and discourses that it could have been identified as his independently of any superscription or tradition. The only direction in which doubt could enter would be in the possible case of a commentary made up, say, by an affectionate disciple, from Ephrem's works with some amalgamated matter from other sources and published under Ephrem's name.

There are some things in the Commentary which appear to invite the supposition, and when we remark that an actual disciple of Ephrem, named Mar Abbā, is credited with a commentary on the Gospel, we may very well ask whether there is any reason to suppose two commentaries on the Gospel to have been written in such close literary proximity. Is it possible that the Commentary of Mar Abbā is the same as the Ephrem Commentary?

The answer must, however, be in the negative. There are a number of extracts from the Commentary of Mar Abbā preserved in the British Museum MS. Add. 17,194, but, while they shew some dependence upon Ephrem, as is natural in the work of a pupil, they shew also remarkable independence.

As nothing of Mar Abbā has been published, as far as I know, and he ranks amongst the earliest Syrian fathers, I transcribe some sentences.

(Cod. Add. 17,194, fol. 48 b.)

ܪܝܫܐ ܐܠܐ ܬܠܡܝܕܗ ܕܡܪܝ ܐܦܪܝܡ ܡܢ

ܦܘܫܩܐ ܕܐܘܢܓܠܝܘܢ . ܗܘܐ ܕܝܢ ܟܕ ܡܟܗܢ ܗܘܐ

i.e. of Mar Abbā, the disciple of Mar Ephrem, from the Commentary on the Gospel. *It came to pass, as he was ministering in the order and custom of the priests,* either for a month of days or from time to time; from the words that *he brought incense* [into the Sanctuary] it was in the seventh month and on the tenth day of the month which is the day of their fast and humiliation. It is likely that he said that he was *among the priests* of the very year of the birth of our Lord; from this seventh month, therefore, which is the former Teshrin in which John was announced, it is known that in the month Nisan was the conception of him whose birth was in the month Canun, on account of what the angel said to Mary, This is the sixth month to her that is called barren.

The reader will notice the agreement with Ephrem in the dates assigned. But the identification of the day that the Angel appeared to Zacharias with the Day of Atonement, does not seem to be expressly made in Ephrem.

(Fol. 59 a.)

ܪܝܫܐ ܐܠܐ ܬܠܡܝܕܗ ܕܡܪܝ ܐܦܪܝܡ ܡܢ ܦܘܫܩܐ

ܕܐܘܢܓܠܝܘܢ . ܐ ܕܝܢ ܟܠܗ ܕܪܫܐ . ܗܘ ܕܝܢ

ܐܢ ܫܘܦܪܐ ܕܩܪܝܒ ܠܟ ܡܟܫܠ ܠܟ ܦܣܘܩܘ.
ܘܫܕܝܗܝ ܡܢܟ. ܦܩܚ ܠܟ ܕܕܠܐ ܚܒܝܒܟ ܘܡܦܪܢܣܢܟ
ܘܫܩܘܠ ܝܘܩܪܟ ܬܥܘܠ ܠܡܠܟܘܬܐ. ܘܠܐ ܕܐܢܬ ܘܗܢܘܢ
ܬܐܙܠܘܢ ܠܢܘܪܐ. ܒܗ̈ܕܡܐ ܕܡܢ ܕܦܣܩ (l. ܕܦܣܝܩ) ܠܢ
ܦܩܚܘܗܝ. ܠܪܚܡܐ ܗܘ ܕܡܣܟܠܢܐ ܐܦܚܡ ܒܗܘܢ.

i.e. of Mar Abbā, disciple of Mar Ephrem, from the Commentary on the Gospel. *If thy right eye*: i.e. if beauty that is near to thee makes thee to err, *cut it off and cast it from thee; it is profitable for thee* that without thy beloved and thy administrator and burden-bearer *thou shouldst enter the kingdom* and not that thou and they *depart into the fire*. With the members whose excision is useful to us he compares the injurious friend.

A reference to the corresponding interpretation from Ephrem, printed on p. 50, will shew that this is quite an independent piece of work.

The same is true of the following extract.

(Fol. 74 b.)

ܕܡܪܝ ܐܒܐ ܬܠܡܝܕܗ ܕܡܪܝ ܐܦܪܝܡ [ܡܢ]
ܦܘܫܩܐ ܕܐܘܢܓܠܝܘܢ. ܠܐ ܬܬܠܘܢ ܩܘܕܫܐ ܠܟ̈ܠܒܐ
ܘܠܐ ܬܪܡܘܢ ܡܪ̈ܓܢܝܬܐ ܩܕܡ ܚܙܝ̈ܪܐ. ܠܡܒ̈ܙܚܢܝ
ܒܟܪܘܙܘܬܐ ܚܕܬܐ ܩܪܐ ܟܠ̈ܒܐ ܘܚܙܝ̈ܪܐ. ܕܡܟܝܠܐ ܕܝܢ
ܕܟܗ̈ܢܐ ܘܦܪ̈ܝܫܐ. ܗܢܘܢ ܕܒܬܪ ܡܠܦܢܘܬܐ ܕܐܠܦܘ
ܗܘܘ ܫ̈ܠܝܚܐ. ܓܕܦܘ ܗܘܘ ܘܚܒܫܘ ܠܫ̈ܠܝܚܐ.

i.e. of Mar Abbā, the disciple of Mar Ephrem, from the Commentary on the Gospel. *Do not give the holy to the dogs, nor cast the pearls before the swine*: he calls those who mocked at the new preaching dogs and swine; likely they were the priests and Pharisees, who after the teaching that the Apostles taught, blasphemed and imprisoned the Apostles.

Probably this will suffice to shew the difference between the Abbā Commentary and the Ephrem Commentary[1].

[1] An interesting question arises whether Abbā's Commentary was also on the Diatessaron. Our extracts include Matthew and Luke: and as it is *à priori* unlikely that Abbā commented on the whole series of Gospels, this is in favour of a belief that the text commented on was a Harmony. But further it will be noticed that in the second extract, the text of Matt. v. 29 is expanded by the words 'that thou shouldest enter the kingdom,' which appears to be Mark ix. 47. There seems to be

So far as Abbâ is concerned, the supposition that the Commentary is the work of a pupil of Ephrem breaks down. But there remains the further question whether perhaps some other disciple may have used up his master's materials in making a Commentary. But here we are in the region of pure speculation, and had better turn back to more solid ground.

This hypothesis, that the Commentary is the work of a disciple, differs so little from that which directly ascribes the composition of the whole series of comments to Ephrem, that it may safely be left for further consideration until such time as the book is worthily edited and honoured with a scientific analysis of the method of its composition.

With this possible reservation, we may ascribe the Commentary to Ephrem, and the reader will have noticed for himself how many strands there are in the evidence for the authorship: if it was not Ephrem's work, almost the whole Syrian Church was deceived in the matter, and they were, of all people, the ones that were likely to know. On this point, then, it is superfluous to say more at present.

Nor is it necessary to multiply words with regard to the text that underlies the Commentary: for, while it is true that there is some confusion in the later Syrian fathers in the statements which they make with regard to the Diatessaron of Tatian and Ephrem's use of it, and this confusion may, perhaps, be a little more widespread than has been hitherto imagined, still, on tracing the various statements to their earliest forms, we find that all confusion disappears, and we have a consistent body of evidence as to the identification of Tatian's Harmony with the Gospel of the Mehallete or Combined Gospels to which the Syrian fathers refer. A pretty instance of fresh evidence will be found on p. 19, where a curious reading is ascribed by one father to the Diatessaron and by another to the Mehallete, where a comparison of the statements made will shew that the same work is intended. But it is unnecessary to spend time in elaborating the argument for the identification of the text of Tatian with that commented on by Ephrem.

I now proceed to draw attention to one or two supplementary

some reason for the suggestion that Abbâ was also working on the Diatessaron, even though the evidence be too slight to decide the question definitely. (Note also *Evangelium* in the singular number.)

matters which come up in connexion with the preceding investigation : and first of all, with regard to the extracts which Isho'dad makes from Ephrem, which are not to be found in the Commentary on the Gospel.

I find, on reference to the Questions of Isho' bar Nun on the Scriptures, of which a copy is in the S.P.C.K. collection[1], that this father makes a number of solutions to the proposed difficulties in the Gospels by reference to the works of Ephrem. And two curious features present themselves : one, that he never seems to quote the Commentary of Ephrem on the Gospel ; the other, that he makes a number of extracts which are very like the unidentified passages from Ephrem in the pages of Isho'dad, and appear to be derived from a common collection of Ephrem extracts. It will thus appear that Isho' bar Nun was not acquainted with the Commentary of Ephrem, or at all events had no access to a copy when he was writing his book of Questions ; while, on the other hand, he had access to other matter taken from Ephrem which was of the nature of a collection of Comments on the Gospel.

For example, in the MS. referred to, we find as follows :

(Fol. 84 r.)

This is almost exactly the quotation which we have printed on p. 23.

And the next question in Isho' bar Nun relates to a question which is discussed shortly after by Isho'dad as to the reason why Pilate's wife did not tell her dream ; concerning which he remarks as follows :

ܒܫܠܡܐ ܟܠܠܐ. ܘܐܫܬܠܡ ܠܗ ܠܒܢܬ ܕܝܢܐ ܒܐܘܪܫܠܡ.
ܬܫܡܫܬܐ ܢܦܠ ܥܠܘܗܝ. ܘܥܠ ܥܠܘܗܝ ܗܘܘ ܕܡܫܡܫܝܢ.

The last part of this extract agrees nearly with the closing words of Isho'dad's extract from Ephrem which we have printed on p. 23; but it is clear that Isho'dad could not have taken it directly from Isho' bar Nun.

One more instance shall be given of the use of some common collection by these two fathers:

On f. 90 r. Isho' bar Nun discourses of the Samaritan woman, as follows:

ܡܪܝ ܐܦܪܝܡ ܕܝܢ ܐܡܪ. ܕܐܢܬܬܐ ܗܝ ܟܠ
ܕܬܬܢܣܒ ܠܗ̇ ܡܢܬ. ܘܗܘܢ ܒܕܡܘܬܐ ܠܡܫܝܚܐ. ܘܐܬܦܪܢܣܬ
ܡܢ ܓܒܪܐ ܗܢܐ ܘܡܠܠܬ ܒܓܒܪ̈ܐ. ܘܕܚܠܬ ܐܚܪ̈ܢܐ
ܕܢܣܒܘܢܝܗ̇ ܒܢܓ̈ܐ. ܘܡܛܠ ܕܒܒܢܬ ܫܡܪ̈ܝܐ ܚܫܝܒܐ
ܗܘܬ ܕܬܬܒ ܐܢܬܬܐ ܕܠܐ ܓܒܪܐ ܦܪܘܬ ܐܢܬܬܐ ܗܝ
ܠܘܬ ܐܚܕ ܡܢ ܗܘܘ ܘܐܬܡܪܬ ܠܗ. ܕܢܬܦܪܐ ܫܡܥܝܢ
ܥܠ ܐܝܟ ܕܒܒܢܬ ܫܡܪ̈ܝܐ. ܘܠܐ ܬܬܦܪܥ ܠܝ ܐܝܟ
ܕܬܫܡܫܬ. ܘܥܠ ܗܕܐ ܐܡܪ ܠܘܬܗ̇ ܦܘܩܕܢܐ ܘܩܪܝ:

This extract should be compared with the following from Isho'dad, fol. 259 r.;

ܡܪܝ ܐܦܪܝܡ. ܗܠܝܢ ܠܡ ܫܡܥܐ ܒܟܠܝܢ ܕܢܣܒܬ
ܚܕ ܒܬܪ ܚܕ ܡܫܐܬ ܗܘܐ. ܗܝ ܕܝܢ ܐܫܬܟܚܬ ܕܐܢܬܬܐ
ܗܝ ܡܛܠ ܒܥܠܐ. ܐܝܟ ܕܐܫܬܟܚܬ ܬܫܪܐ ܠܡܫܘܕܝܐ
ܕܥܠܘܗܝ ܠܥܠܡܐ ܡܢ ܫܘܒܬܗ̇. ܘܡܛܠ ܕܢܫܝܐ ܗܘܬ
ܐܪܡܠܬܐ. ܐܬܦܪܫܬ ܘܢܣܒܬ ܚܕ.... ܕܬܬܦܪܐ ܒܟܠܗ̇
ܟܠܝܢ ܘܢܣܒܪ ܢܫܝܗ̇.

The common matter in these two traditions is evident, and both writers profess to be retailing Ephrem; but it is not the Commentary that they quote, if we may judge from the Armenian.

We suspect then that both writers have access to some other

Commentary on the Gospels in which Ephrem is freely quoted, or to some collection of extracts from Ephrem.

I pass on in the next place to consider some curious coincidences between the Ephrem Commentary and the Commentaries of the Venerable Bede, which suggest that the extreme East and West are in contact at some unknown Patristic point.

In his Commentary on Luke c. 1, (ed. Giles, Vol. i. p. 280), Bede says :

Joannes ergo interpretatur in quo est gratia, vel Domini gratia.

Cf. Mösinger, p. 12. Joannes, quod nomen indicat, nos misericordia indigere.

Bede (p. 284). *Et occultabat se mensibus quinque* etc....Elisabeth...de ipsis quae accipere cupiebat donis erubescit, et licet de ablato gaudeat opprobrio sterilitatis, de partu tamen anilis verecundatur aetatis.

Cf. Mösinger, p. 15 ut supra.

Bede (p. 287). De utroque potest intelligi, quod dicitur de domo David.

Cf. Mösinger, p. 16. Alio loco eadem Scriptura dixit, utrumque, Josephum et Mariam, esse ex domo David.

The interpretation of Bede coincides with that of Tatian, Ephrem, and the Sinai Syriac.

Bede (p. 293). *Et intravit in domum Zachariae, et salutavit Elisabeth....* Maria ad Elisabeth, Dominus venit ad Joannem...majorumque humiliatio minorum est utique exaltatio.

Cf. Mösinger, p. 17. Maria surgens abiit ad Elisabeth, quae minor ea erat, sicut et Dominus ad Joannem venit.

Bede (p. 345). *Et ne coeperitis dicere, patrem habemus Abraham, etc.* Quid enim lapides...Nec immerito lapidum nomine gentes significatae sunt, quae lapides coluerunt ; unde scriptum est, Similes illis fiant qui faciunt et omnes qui confidunt in eis.

Cf. Mösinger, p. 40. *Ex lapidibus istis*...ex adoratoribus lapidum et lignorum.

Bede (p. 346). Et notandum securim non juxta ramos positam, sed ad radicem dicit.

Cf. Mösinger, p. 39. Et perdet ramos sylvae securi, dixit Isaias. Ramos dixit, non radices....Usque ad radicem arboris, quod Isaias praetermiserat.

Bede (p. 391). Et vidit duas naves stantes secus stagnum. Duae naves secus stagnum positae, circumcisionem et praeputium figurant.

Cf. Mösinger, p. 59. Duae naves sunt circumcisio et praeputium.

Bede (p. 393). Mergi naves est, homines in seculum, ex quo elati per fidem fuerant, morum pravitate relabi.

Cf. Mösinger (p. 59). Quibus verbis doctrina Prophetarum significatur, de excelso missa in mundum, qui per mare repraesentatus est.

Bede (Vol. ii. p. 143). Immundus quippe spiritus exiit a Judaeis, quando acceperunt legem. Et ambulavit per loca arida quaerens sibi requiem. Expulsus, videlicet, a Judaeis, ambulavit per gentium solitudines.

Cf. Mösinger (p. 121). Quum Deus eis salvatorem misisset, qui eos educeret (sc. ex Aegypto), ille immundus aufugit et sanati sunt...Ille igitur immundus ex eis expulsus transivit per loca arida, i.e. per gentes.

An examination of the foregoing parallels will shew curious agreement in the underlying ideas, as well as actual coincidences of language and of text. The question is, What does the community of ideas imply? A reference to the sources from which Bede draws his comments will help us to take the first step in the solution of the problem. We gather from his dedicatory letter to Acca that he drew upon Ambrose, Augustine, Gregory the Great, &c. And the last named is undoubtedly responsible for a number of the sentences quoted above. For example, in Gregory's twentieth Homily on the Gospel, we find the sentence 'nec immerito lapidum nomine gentes significatae sunt, quia lapides coluerunt, unde scriptum est: Similes illis fiant qui faciunt ea et omnes qui confidunt in eis,' which is almost *verbatim* and *literatim* what we have above in Bede.

In the same Homily the words "Securim non juxta ramos positam sed ad radicem dicit" go over without change into Bede.

We may conclude that some (if not all) of the coincidence which we detect between the early Eastern and late Western commentaries is due to the use of extracts from the works of Gregory the Great. What then are the common sources of Ephrem and Gregory, or does Gregory borrow from Ephrem? This is a more difficult question to answer. But we may see some of the difficulties disappear if we observe that much of the common matter under discussion is earlier than Ephrem. For example, compare the extract from Bede, in which he explains what are the stones of which children are to be raised up to Abraham, with the following passage from Origen's 22nd Homily on Luke:

De quibus lapidibus? Non utique lapides irrationabiles corporeosque monstrabat, sed homines insensibiles et quondam duros, qui quia lapides et ligna adorabant, impletum est illud quod in psalmo cantabatur: 'Similes illis fiunt qui faciunt ea et omnes qui confidunt eis.'

The coincidence is now not one between Bede (i.e. Gregory) and Ephrem, but between Origen and Ephrem.

Now the reader has probably noticed that most of the coincidences to which we have drawn attention above are due to interpretations of a very simple character, constituting a sort of Targum on the text, like the equation between ‘the two ships’ and ‘the two peoples,’ and the like.

And it admits of demonstration that these glosses are of very high antiquity; take, for example, the explanation that the *sea* stands for the *world*, which is a favourite with Ephrem. We find the same explanation underlying the passage in Aphraates (col. 41),

Nolite haesitare, ne demergamini *in mundum*, velut Simon, qui cum dubitasset, demergi coepit *in mare;*

a passage, by the bye, which Zahn seems to us to have too hastily carried back into the Diatessaron, without detaching the gloss from the text.

We suspect then that there is a primitive Targum on the Gospel, from which this and similar glosses come : and the very same thing is suggested by such passages as that quoted on p. 72 from Moses bar Kepha, where the writer is in parallelism with Ephrem, but betrays their common source to be a succinct Commentary upon Matthew. And indeed Origen himself implies the existence of such primitive commentaries in a remarkable passage in his 34th Homily on Luke.

Aiebat quidam de presbyteris volens parabolam interpretari, hominem qui descendit esse Adam, Jerusalem paradisum ; Jericho, mundum[1]; latrones, contrarias fortitudines; sacerdotem, legem ; Levitam, prophetas; Samaritam, Christum ; vulnera vero, inobedientiam ; animal, corpus Domini ; pandochium [id est stabulum][2], quod universos volentes introire suscipiat, Ecclesiam interpretari.

Here, then, we have an actual specimen of an early Targum ; and the influence may be felt in Patristic literature. For example, Bede (ii. 126) begins his interpretation of the parable as follows :

Homo iste, Adam intelligitur in genere humano, Hierusalem, civitas pacis illa caelestis, a cujus beatitudine lapsus, in hanc mortalem miseramque vitam devenit ;

and goes on

plagae, peccata sunt... ; jumentum ejus est caro, etc. ;

through which it is easy to see the shining of the primitive interpretation.

---

[1] Hence, perhaps, Marcion’s theory that our Lord descended at Jericho: cf. Barnes in *Academy*, Oct. 20, 1893.

[2] Ruffinus’ explanation?

A volume might be written on the persistence of such early elucidations.

We suspect, then, as we have said, that it is to such a primitive Targum of the Presbyters that we are to look for the explanation of many of the coincidences in interpretations and glosses between Eastern and Western, and Syrian and non-Syrian fathers. The subject is an interesting one, and demands a closer examination. For the present we content ourselves with making suggestions as to the method of pursuing the enquiry, and prophecies as to its probable result.

Since writing the foregoing lines I have seen Goussen's just published Apocalypsis Versio Sahidica, to which is appended a collection of extracts from the Diatessaron taken from a MS. of Ishoʿdad at Berlin (Cod. Sachau 311). Goussen adds to our collection a passage from the beginning of a Comm. on the Acts of the Apostles which gives the names of the twelve Apostles as they stood in the Diatessaron. (My copy of Ishoʿdad is confined to the Four Gospels.)

The extract is as follows:

ܒܕܝܛܛܪܘܢ ܗܟܢܐ. ܫܡܥܘܢ ܕܐܬܩܪܝ ܟܐܦܐ.
ܘܐܢܕܪܐܘܣ ܐܚܘܗܝ. ܘܝܥܩܘܒ ܘܝܘܚܢܢ ܒܢ̈ܝ ܙܒܕܝ.
ܘܦܝܠܝܦܘܣ ܘܒܪ ܬܘܠܡܝ. ܘܬܐܘܡܐ ܘܡܬܝ ܡܟܣܐ.
ܘܝܥܩܘܒ ܠܒܝܐ ܒܪ ܚܠܦܝ. ܘܫܡܥܘܢ ܩܢܢܝܐ.
ܘܝܗܘܕܐ ܒܪ ܝܥܩܘܒ ܘܝܗܘܕܐ ܣܟܪܝܘܛܐ ܗܘ ܕܗܘܐ
ܡܫܠܡܢܐ.

an arrangement of the names which, as Zahn points out (*Theol. Lit.-Blatt*, Oct. 18, 1895), has influenced the text of the Lewis Codex in Matt. x.

Cambridge:

PRINTED BY J. AND C. F. CLAY,

AT THE UNIVERSITY PRESS.